RUTHLESS WOLF

BLACK DIAMOND ALPHA 1

A FOREVER MATES TRILOGY

TALA MOORE

FOREVER MATES

CONTENTS

CHAPTER 1

LUKE

My kind does their best to slip under the radar, and while I questioned this principle growing up, I realize now it's a protective measure for our sanity just as much for our physical safety.

If shifters documented every detail of their lives on social media like humans, my memories would announce that on this day my entire family was slaughtered right in front of me.

While I stood by and watched.

"Give me your best bourbon on the rocks," I call out to the bartender.

"What's the occasion?" the bartender asks as he unearths a jewel-encrusted bottle.

I hesitate. Death. Loss. The drive for justice. "Anniversary."

"Well, happy anniversary man! You'll have to bring in your old lady sometime. We get a bit rowdy, but we do protect our women here."

I tip my glass up to the bartender, wondering if I'll taste anything beyond the bitterness coating my tongue. "I'm sure you do."

Can he detect the malice slipping through? The hard edges

to my words? If he does, he doesn't show it. My throat burns with the drink and the growing lump in my throat.

I watch the sweet fiery liquid spin in the glass much like the black hole of my own mind, wondering if I should fight the pull but knowing there's no point.

The memories are burnt in there for a reason. Branded.

They're demanding justice.

I t's a hot, humid day up at the pack's compound. Gathered for a true celebration, my lips graze the jawline of my mate, only pulling free to listen as my dad calls everyone's attention.

"Listen up, everyone!" my father, our pack leader, bellows.

And when an Alpha commands, you obey. There's no room for disobedience in a pack. We immediately grow silent, my mate lowering her head because celebration or not, my father's an intimidating man.

"As you know, we've all gathered here today to welcome the return of our very own prodigal son, Joel."

We howl out to the surrounding woods and beyond that to the full moon. Our cheering is somewhere between pure joy and a strange primal relief. In the same way animals cry when their young are taken away, we mourned Joel's disappearance. Now, we're rejoicing in his return even more.

My mate squeezes my hands. My brother's violent streak and rebellion against the shifter ways didn't leave much room for hope that he would return.

"You can take the shifter out of the wild," our father cries out, pulling Joel in, "but you can never take the wild out of the shifter. They always come back."

My sisters and brothers throw back their heads and howl once more, their bodies restless under the full moon and this new energy. A *revival. Renewal. Even my own skin has been crawling for hours, ready to shed this human husk for something more comfortable. Joel makes his way through the crowd, grinning through the back slaps and jostles.*

He reaches me and I draw him in for a hug. We hold each other for long seconds, memories of a childhood spent roaming the woods and getting up to mischief reminding us that our bond has always been a strong one. No matter what.

Somehow, despite all the conflict, uncertainty, and countless pack meetings where my dad stressed the importance of never leaving and the high price it costs to return after such a betrayal, there's no ill will. It's as if all was forgotten. Animals are like that, though. We don't hold grudges against our own.

Joel pulls back. "And who is this? How did you secure Miss Rosie Mae as a mate, hm?" He looks over at her. "I thought you had better taste than this." He winks at her, and when she blushes I'm reminded that the two had a small summer fling a few years ago.

A small, uncontrollable snarl slips between my lips. Joel only laughs and Rosie Mae weaves her fingers through mine, whispering that we are bound.

"You have nothing to worry about."

Her murmurs immediately calm the beast within. I'm about to suggest we go grab a drink—there are two years of missed time to catch up on—when my father demands our attention once more. I move closer to Rose Mae as she cowers. He's our Alpha, yes, but it's always tugged at my heart to see my sweet girl so scared, like a pup with her tail between her legs.

Then again, we're all scared of my dad. That's just how it is when you're in a pack. Looking back, I wonder if he regrets what he said that night.

If there's an afterlife, does he feel guilty?

"Last year, my son Joel declared his hatred of our kind. For his own self. He broke my heart, his mama's heart, and destroyed this

pack collectively. He was a vital part of our pack, and I ain't just sayin' that cause he's my son. I would feel it just as deeply if any of y'all abandoned us. Our bloodlines and our power bind us in ways we will never be bound to someone in the outside world. Joel put all of us at risk. The only way we survive is together. No outsiders. No minglin' with other shifters who don't respect us. We are the strongest pack in these parts because of our loyalty."

He pauses for so long that I think the speech is over. Even Rose Mae starts to lift her hands to clap.

But he continues. "I know there won't be a next time, but if there is, whether it's Joel or any of you, there will be severe consequences. You will not be welcomed back. If any of you," he pauses again, looking directly at Joel before continuing, "betray the pack again, you will be dead to me."

Those were the last words he ever spoke.

The harsh silence that followed his statement was punctured by a cry. An unnatural, gurgled, animalistic one.

Joel once left us because he was afraid of the beast within, but it was never his inner beast he had to fear. It was others.

I don't know what I expected to see when I turned around. Maybe some crazy human? Maybe old man Thomas was having a stroke. I never expected a group of unfamiliar shifters to snatch up my pack mates.

Claws ripped my brother's and sister's flesh from their bodies, their rabid tongues licking up the overflow of blood. There were so many of them. Everywhere. Death a promise in their hungry eyes.

I'd pulled Rosie Mae behind me as one of the giant wolves leapt up at us. Her chilling scream will haunt me until the day I die. Her limp body fell to the ground as I turned to see if she was okay. Another wolf was standing over her. It curled it's lip at me before darting away, looking for another easy kill

Blood. There was so much blood. Her eyes were glazed as if

looking into a place none of us will ever see, each spasm of her body indicating she was gone.

"No!"

My bones had melted into me as I started to shift, but something hot squeezed my wrist. "Joel!"

"Brother, you need to run." He'd pulled my body down behind a bush. "Run, and never ever look back, okay? I should've never returned... We're outnumbered, and you're too young to fight, Luke."

"Then run with me!" I'd whimpered, unable to understand what was happening. We were celebrating. And now this... "Don't make me leave you."

"You need to survive. Continue our lineage. Get as many as you can to follow you."

I remember how weak his hug was. How every feature was twisted with desperation. He was already injured.

He didn't believe he'd survive, even if he left with me.

His last action was to push me. Shove me away from the fighting and bloodshed. Away from my pack.

Running as blindly as I'd followed my brother's order, I'd screamed for the others to follow me.

I grip the tumbler, sneering when I find it's empty.

As empty as my heart has been since that night.

No one followed me. Why would they? Shifters don't leave their pack behind. Yet I'd run and run for what must've been hours until I collapsed by the creek in another town. I squeeze my eyes tightly shut. As I went to drink the cold water, I swore I could see Rosie Mae's reflection looking back at me.

I went back to search for survivors. Survivors who didn't exist. Most of the bodies were unidentifiable, but I saw Rosie

Mae's bracelet on a severed arm just as I spotted my dad's dog tags.

I'd curled up next to what remained of my parent's bodies. The hours that followed were a blur, and to this day, I can't remember most of it. I only remember the tears of both my wolf and human consuming me until the rising sun warmed my shivering body.

Then I stood up in the center of the carnage. I knew what I had to do. What any decent son of an Alpha would do. I made a promise to my ancestors, any god which may be listening, and the blood-soaked ground on which I stood.

"You will pay for this."

I was never able to return home after that. I knew they'd be watching. Leaving behind everything I knew, I tracked down an old family friend. They weren't a shifter or part of the pack, but they were trusted.

Graciously, she took me in as her own. "I don't know a lot about these things, but I do know your ma and pa would've wanted you safe. Come in, let's get you cleaned up."

Inside the living area, she had a needlework sign that read "time heals all wounds."

Bull-fucking-shit. Five years later and here I am, at a bar filled with the people who slaughtered my family, as I wait silently for an opening into their little group.

A wolf in sheep's clothing, ready to infiltrate and destroy when they least expect it.

Across the bar, one of the rival pack's most outgoing members throws back a beer and begins dancing. A familiar, sickening weight settles like rocks in my stomach, and it takes every ounce of self-control not to rip him apart right here, right now. These are the monsters who killed my family. In the endless days that have passed, they've blissfully lived their lives, gyrating, drinking, working, having children, falling in love, and every damn thing I stopped wanting on that fateful day.

For me, time couldn't heal my wounds. It stopped.

Waiting. Breath held.

The rocks in my stomach continue to pile up, heavy and jagged. Yet, the moment I look up, they transform into butterflies.

It's her.

All legs and curves and innocence, she's a stark contrast to the hard edges and wickedness we're surrounded by. In all the time I've been watching her, I can't figure out why she's here. How could someone so seemingly harmless be part of such a vicious pack?

I shake myself mentally. She may look like sweetness personified, but she's one of *them*.

The enemy.

More than that, that sheltered naivety is their weakness. My in.

Although I don't intend to, my eyes roam up her body. Lean legs, sultry hips, tits that make my mouth dry, a mouth that I've seen from afar, but now realize it's lush in a way that instantly tightens my gut. Trying to snap myself out of whatever the fuck is happening, I yank my eyes to hers.

And stop.

Vivid blue captures me. Swallows me. And holds me in a way I've never been held.

They connect with something deep. Maybe it's something I thought died five years ago. Or maybe it's something that may not have existed until this moment.

Just like this girl, it's sweet. Beautiful. Too good to be possible.

But also hot. And aching. And electrifying.

I yank my gaze away, even as I curse myself. What the fuck

is wrong with me? I should be jumping on the attraction that just crackled like lightning. Instead, I'm back to gazing at the bottom of my glass. Seems I'm too sober for this. Or maybe it's because I've been so isolated that I only know how to communicate with a fifty-year-old woman about her latest crafting project.

Sifting through pickup lines in my head—that's what human men do, right?—I nearly jump when she whispers in my ear. "What's a guy like you doin' in a bar like this?"

I look up, steeling myself this time. The crackle of energy is there as our eyes connect, but I keep my head on enough to realize something.

She's making a move on me.

So much for sweet and innocent. I knew it was all an act.

The knowledge instantly realigns my equilibrium. I can play this game. And I might even enjoy it.

"Adeline, don't go wastin' your time on this man," the bartender interrupts. "He's here celebratin' his anniversary."

"Oh," she says, her perfect mouth forming a delicious 'o.' Her hands flutter to her throat before she quickly drops them. She throws her black waterfall of hair over her shoulder. "Is that so?" She lifts my glass of bourbon to her nose, and shakes her head after taking a quick sniff. "More like a divorce. Bourbon? Really?"

Opening my mouth, I pause when she grabs my hands. "And no ring. Now most men when they cheat on their women don't go announcing that it's their anniversary."

"Good point," the bartender agrees, raising an eyebrow at me.

I flash a smile, hoping it has more warmth to it than I feel. "It's actually the anniversary of my dad's death." Every lie must have a bit of truth to it. "A bad car accident a few years ago."

"Shit man, I'm sorry! I just assumed," the bartender says. "Your next drink is on me, okay?"

"It's no big deal," I mutter, shrugging a shoulder.

"Is that why you're sad?" Adeline murmurs quietly.

I spin to face her, realizing she still has my hand in hers. "What?" I demand, my voice harsh in a way it shouldn't be. I'm doing a shit job of making a move on her.

A smile hovers on her lips, even as her blue eyes stay serious. "Like attracts like."

For the second time in the last few minutes, I can't hold her gaze. Instead, I look down at our joined hands. This is going better than I could've ever planned, so why does a part of me want to get up and run faster than I ever have in my life?

Slowly, almost hesitantly, Adeline interlaces her fingers through mine, her touch sending electric shivers through my body. She's telling me she doesn't want me to go.

She's asking me to stay.

Which is what I came here to do.

Just like that, the butterflies drop dead. They change back to rocks as I remember my vow to my pack.

I push to my feet. "Let's dance," I growl, even as I wait to see if she'll agree.

A mischievous look glints in her eyes as if she's doing something naughty—as if this is forbidden. Does she know who I am? Maybe it's because she thinks I'm human...

And then she tugs me toward the half-lit dance floor. She stops in the center, music pulsing around us as she guides my hands to her hips. As we begin to sway, I have to remind myself that I'm here to seduce her, not the other way around.

This beautiful, wide-eyed shifter may hide behind her innocent charm, but I know exactly what kind of monster she and her brothers are. Evil courses through her veins. This seductive play is proof of that. She doesn't even know my name and yet her eyes are already filling with all the things she wants me to do to her body.

I jerk her in close, pushing my arousal against her so she can see exactly what she's doing to me. I'm rewarded with a startled breath, then a supple melting of her body against mine, as if she's already welcoming me inside. A growl instinctively climbs up my throat and my fingers dig into her hips, exploring the boundaries of how far I can go with a female shifter in the open, surrounded by her pack mates.

I'm all too aware of the hostile gazes and soft growls in the room from wolves who have no idea my intentions go far beyond the moans I intend to elicit from her body. From wolves who would've ripped me to shreds long ago if they knew who I was.

Adeline shudders delicately, looking up at me with wide eyes as we continue our dangerous dance.

A dance that will end with her death.

And the blood of her family on my hands.

CHAPTER 2

ADELINE

Being a female in a family of possessive wolves—actual wolves—isn't a walk in the sun. It's more like a walk in a hurricane. Trudging through the onslaught of the storm. While chained to my brothers who act as if they are protecting me when all they're doing is locking me away in a tower as if I'm Rapunzel.

What they don't know is that every time they insist I stay in and "be safe" they're only pushing me right out my bedroom window, as if I'm still a teenager, and right into the very place they deem unsafe. Moonlit, the bar that my pack frequents.

For a moment, I consider going somewhere else, only to know I won't. As pathetic as it is, Moonlit is as far as my rebellion goes—a bar where everyone knows me. Beyond that are all the dangers my parents and brothers are always telling stories about. All the dangers they tell me I'm not strong enough to face. Although I tell myself I don't believe them, I also haven't tested their theory...

Stealthily, I slip out of my window and land almost silently on the grass in our backyard. Surrounding me are countless other homes that my pack-mates live in. One day, I'll be living in one of these with my mate, popping out pups and living under the watchful eye of the Alpha. I could gag if I wasn't trying to be so quiet and sneak off unnoticed.

One step at a time, I tell myself. Then I'll see if there's a world beyond the boundaries of my pack.

I throw my hair over my shoulder and adjust the straps on my tank top. It's my skimpiest outfit, which really isn't all that skimpy, because heaven knows my parents would never allow for that much of me to show. It would draw attention. Gritting my teeth, I push open the door to the bar. I love them, I do, but sometimes I wonder if life would be easier had I not been born a shifter.

I take one step inside and stop.

Jake arches a brow as he straightens from the billiard table he was about to execute a move on. "Addy?"

Of all the people to run into...

Pack loyalty is drilled into our heads since we're just pups. But there are loopholes and places where the definitions of this loyalty shift. Moonlit is one of those places. Sure, everyone knows that sweet, innocent Adeline isn't supposed to be at the bar, but they also know that if I'm here, I'm not sneaking off elsewhere. They know just as much as I do that Moonlit is where I can run away to, without actually running away.

Although none of that matters to my family. Just like it doesn't matter that I'm an adult and definitely over the drinking age. And Jake may be my favorite brother and the one closest in age, but he's still family.

I jut my chin. "I'm stopping in for a drink."

He leans against his pool cue. "And what are you gonna do when Dad shows up to do the same?"

My gaze frantically darts around the gloomy bar. "Dad would never!" I gasp, hating the instant desire to hightail it straight back to my room.

Jake grins, then leans back over the pool table. "He doesn't come here on Fridays. And if anyone asks, I didn't on this particular one, either."

Flashing him a grateful smile, I relax. I'm actually going to get a chance to catch up with a few of the friends I've barely seen since they were mated. My eyes roam around the bar, this time actually registering the patrons rather than frantically looking for my father's disappointed scowl.

This time when I freeze, I forget to move. Breathe. And wonder absentmindedly whether it even matters.

A man is sitting at the bar, alone and gazing into his drink. His profile reveals thick waves of dark blonde hair falling over his forehead, messy and tousled. A strong nose. Chiseled lips. Muscles in all the right places.

He's deliciously hot, but that's not the only thing that has me captivated. There's something about him...

Maybe it's because he's not a part of my pack. Or because his shoulders are hunched ever so slightly, as if he doesn't want them to be, but his body isn't listening. Or because loneliness clings to him in the same way the shadows do.

I'm moving before I've even realized it. I know I shouldn't approach another man outside of the shifter community, but dammit, I can't help myself. The need to be closer to him is overwhelming.

He looks up as if he knew I was there, and I draw in a sharp breath as my gaze connects with green eyes the color of spring. Of new beginnings. Of freedom.

Yet it's a glance that has a strange tingling in my gut. No lower... Enough to make me tighten my thighs, trying to hold on to the sensation.

I smile just before he averts his gaze, and the moment our eyes disconnect, I'm left floundering.

I pause, standing there in the middle of the bar as the

seconds claw their way forward. Did I just imagine all that? Hot on the heels of the thought is the knowledge that one look doesn't mean anything. I feel a little stupid. Most definitely naïve.

My family's endless warnings float through my mind.

You're too trusting, Addy. Life ain't no fairytale, you know.

It never occurs to you that people may have a hidden agenda.

Your soft heart will get hurt, and we'll be the ones picking up the pieces.

Each one a reason I shouldn't be here, pretending I'm like anyone else.

My weight shifts, ready to turn back around and leave Moonlit, only to find I don't move. To find that I don't want to leave.

To discover that I have a choice.

I lift my chin. Tonight, I'm not that Addy. I'm whoever I want to be, dammit.

And that woman wants to learn that guy's name. Heck, she wants to dance with him. She wants to explore the heat pooling deep in her groin. That Addy has the courage to make it happen.

Breathing in confidence that I don't possess, I walk up to this mysterious, sad, sexy man and whisper the first line that comes into my head. "What's a guy like you doin' in a bar like this?"

I cringe the moment the words escape my lips, grateful he isn't looking at me. Even if my voice and body language scream 'confident woman', I sure as heck don't feel it. Inhaling, I compose myself as he lifts his head to meet my gaze. Our eyes connect again, and there's that feeling once more.

The ground disappearing beneath me, and I don't freaking care.

"Adeline, don't go wastin' your time on this man," my

favorite cousin and the owner of this bar, interrupts. "He's here celebratin' his anniversary."

My heart drops as the wheels begin to turn. Dammit, Addy! Now I must really look like a fool. Only I refuse to show my embarrassment. I avert my gaze, then pause. There's something about his body language, the absence of a ring, and the fact I can't detect the scent of a woman on his skin. In fact, all I catch is the scent of a cat and that old lady perfume my grandmother wears.

When I meet his gaze once more, those lonely eyes are a clear indicator that he can't possibly be in a relationship. At least not a happy one.

"Is that so?" I purr as if I talk like this all the time. Lifting up his drink, I wrinkle my nose. "More like a divorce!" When I hear a chuckle from my cousin, I realize I spoke my observations out loud. "Bourbon?" I ask, looking at Lonely Eyes, careful to tone my words down with jest. "Really?"

I continue pointing out my discoveries and how he can't possibly be celebrating a wedding anniversary.

My cousin agrees when the mystery man finally speaks. "It's actually the anniversary of my dad's death... A bad car accident a few years ago."

That explains the sadness. It's loss. A loss that's cut deep.

Beside us, my cousin fumbles over himself, his hands jittering with that nervous wolf energy of his as he apologizes, but I barely register it.

"It's no big deal," Lonely Eyes mutters, shrugging a shoulder.

I clench my hands. The urge to touch him is overwhelming. To tell him he doesn't need to pretend with me. Next thing I know, my hand is on his. "Is that why you're sad?"

"What?" he demands, looking like I just punched him in the gut

I almost smile. "Like attracts like."

I've known loneliness. Most of my life has been defined by it. Wondering if I'm going crazy, I interlace my fingers through his. I've never been so bold. Didn't even know I could be. But the feelings swirling through me are undeniable. And so freaking right.

All I know is I don't want them to end.

Lonely Eyes pushes to his feet, his muscled length eclipsing me in the most delicious ways. "Let's dance," he growls in a way that vibrates straight through me. Yet despite the order, he waits, as if to make sure I want this.

Which I most definitely do.

I take his hand and lead him to the dance floor, anticipation thrumming through my veins. Would I be bold enough to kiss him? To find out how he tastes?

I stop in the center, instinct making me take his hands and put them on my hips. They mold to my curves, hot and possessive. And then he jerks me in close and I feel the evidence of his desire. My mouth goes dry. My breath disintegrates. The long heat pressed against my belly calls to something primal in me.

"I didn't catch your name," I breathe, trying to get some semblance of sanity even as I drape my arms around his shoulders.

"Luke," he murmurs. His voice is now soft, unlike the growling demand to dance. As if catching himself, as if his vulnerability is a weakness, his tone shifts back to its harsh tone. "My name is Luke."

He doesn't seem to realize that the rasping tone is the one that speaks to me more. There's a rawness to it, layers that I want to peel back. I've been handled with kid gloves all my life. I don't want gentle.

I pull him closer to me, knowing all too well that all of

Moonlit is watching our dance. It's a dangerous dance. Shifters aren't supposed to mingle with those outside their pack, but dammit I can't stop myself. I feel alive for the first time in my life.

His hands guide my hips in a rhythm against his, and as this song fades and a new one begins, my gaze drops to his lips. They look soft. Yet firm. They part on a hissing breath and my gaze shoots up. Luke's looking at me as if he wants to devour me.

My stomach tightens. My sex clenches. I want to discover all the ways he could consume me.

Several low growls rumble through the crowd, and I know that if I can't at least pull myself away from Luke, we need to get out of Moonlit before my pack lose their temper. "Take me somewhere else," I whisper, trying to make the words sound like a command, but they lack any authority. After all, this isn't like me. I'm not the kind of girl who dances with strangers, let alone asks for more. And I'm sober!

But I bite my lip, heat rising to my cheeks, and manage to lift my head high. I refuse to back down and hide in a corner. How am I ever going to experience life if I keep doing that?

And Luke is something I'd very much like to experience.

His gaze does the impossible and heats. "Quite the seductress, aren't you?"

I lean a little closer. "I am now." That's a word that's never been used to describe me, but I like knowing I'm seducing him as completely as he's seducing me.

Luke's fingers dig into my hips, sending darts of pleasure through my quivering muscles. "Well, it's working. I want to taste you, Adeline."

His hungry gaze fearlessly devours me, and I realize how illicit this must appear to the pack. Yet even if I'm squirming under the scrutiny of my fellow shifters and the uncertainty of this uncharted territory that is Luke—of men in general—I don't want this to end.

I blush. "We should...ah...go." Dammit, now I'm stumbling. I tug at his arm. "My older brothers could come in, and that wouldn't end well."

A strange darkness flashes across Luke's face, and his eyes empty for such a brief moment that I wonder if I imagined it. He lets out a deep grunt before whispering, "I know a place. It's not far away."

I pull back, smiling. "Dinner would be lovely," I say, just a little too loud. "I'm starving."

Luke's eyes heat. "Me, too," he growls, the words seeming to scrape over my sensitive skin.

I avoid everyone's gazes as I head toward the door, surprised that I exit Moonlit without Jake accosting me. He either assumes I'd never lie and am actually heading out to dinner, or he's too shocked by what he's seeing.

Little Addy, picking up.

It's only once we're outside that I hesitate. Nervously biting my lip, I wonder whether I'm ready for this. The most I've ever done with a boy was meet one of my pack-mates at the local make-out spot.

Luke stops behind me, close enough that his chest brushes my back. His heat wraps around me. "I could get a room at the motel next door."

"That's convenient," I breathe, glancing at the plain building that stretches out only a few yards away from Moonlit. I'm pretty sure that's where my brothers take their hookups to.

Luke's breath coasts over my neck, and I think I hear him draw in a deep breath, as if he's inhaling my scent. The thought makes my knees go weak. "God, you smell good."

I can't help myself. I lean back, wanting more heat. More sensation. More words like those, growled like they're a confession. Luke's hands wrap around my waist, pulling me hard against him and I feel his arousal pressing into my ass. Instinctively, I grind my hips backward, closing my eyes as his chest shudders. He's feeling this as intensely as I am. I know he is.

And we haven't even kissed.

I turn in his arms, wanting to remedy that, but a sound from the bar has us both stiffening. Then, Luke's taking my hand and striding toward the motel, and I'm half-running to keep up with him. The warm night air brushes my hair back from my face, cooling my blood. With a hot look, he leaves me in the shadows of a tree as he strides to reception.

Giving me a moment to think.

I'm both thrilled and terrified as I realize I'm doing something that is contrary to who I am—or at least, who I'm expected to be. I didn't think I was going to lose my virginity tonight, much less in a sketchy hotel by a bar I shouldn't have even been at, but here I am. Life is funny that way, and I can't help but bask in every minute of it. It's not often I get to enjoy anything other than domestic tasks and being a "good shifter girl."

Luke's back faster than I expected, his green eyes dark with desire. He takes my hand and pulls me to the nearest room, swipes a card over the sensor of the door and pulls me inside. The action is rough, almost dominant, but it thrills me. He can't get me inside fast enough.

The moment the door's shut, he pushes me against it, pressing the long, hot length of his body against mine. His breath puffs against my lips. His arousal brands me where it presses against the juncture of my thighs, leaving me a shivering mess of desire I didn't know I could be.

I moisten my lips with the tip of my tongue and his gaze is drawn to the motion. "Adeline," he groans softly.

I don't know what he's asking for. Or why he pauses. But

both the question and the hesitation call to something deep in me. For some reason, Luke wants reassurance. And I want to give it to him.

"I want you," I respond, my voice a husky whisper.

My fingers spear into his hair, gripping as I tug his mouth closer. The words, the invite, are all he needs.

Luke's mouth descends on mine, a ravenous, devouring beast. I gasp at the totality of the heat. The sensations. The explosive way my body responds. Our tongues hungrily find the other's, insatiable in their exploration of the other. He tastes faintly of bourbon, overwhelmingly of everything I never knew I was looking for. I can't get enough of it.

"Fuck, Addy," Luke gasps, his hips suddenly moving in the same rhythm as his tongue.

Moisture floods my sex and all I can do is cling to him as his hands greedily explore my body. I've overheard other pack members talk about sex, and I secretly took notes should that day ever come, but everything I thought I would need to know is out the window as my body responds instinctively. I yank off his shirt, wanting to touch him. All of him.

Although it's dark in the motel room, I can still make out the molded shoulders, the rippling chest muscles that move with each of his panting breaths. My hands roam over thick biceps, skim over ridged abdominals that tremble beneath my fingertips, already curious what I'll find below.

Except Luke grabs my hand. "You do that and this will be over far sooner than either of us would like," he growls against my lips.

I mewl a little when he pulls back, but his hands grab the bottom of my tank top and pull it off. I lift my arms, letting him. I desperately want to feel more skin on skin.

Luke's hand goes to the back of my simple, white bra.

Despite the urgency in his touch, he pauses before unclasping. "Is this okay?"

I murmur my approval, arching my back with impatience as if I'm some wanton being. I can barely recognize myself, and yet I revel in this unfurling. This blossoming. A quick snap and my bra is free. Luke yanks it off impatiently, a low sound reverberating in the back of his throat as my breasts are exposed.

His mouth leaves a trail of scorching kisses down my neck before he takes a nipple in his mouth. I arch so quickly my head bangs against the door, although I barely register it. Scorching desire is spearing from where his wet mouth is suckling me straight to my groin. It tugs at something deep. Something that wants to be satisfied.

He worships the other breast, leaving me a mewling mass of passion, before returning to my mouth as if he can't get enough of it. Kissing me deeply, he hauls me up against him, his arm like hot steel around my back. I'm crushed against him, my sensitive breasts plastered against a hard, burning wall of muscle. Even though we're pressed tightly against each other, it doesn't feel close enough. I bring one leg up and wrap it around his waist, then the other, leaving me clinging to him. My sex is against his hot ridge and I can feel him grow as his hips grind into mine.

"I'm trying to go slow, Addy," he groans, sounding as if he's in pain.

"I don't want slow," I gasp. "I want you."

It feels like my body's been starved for Luke all its life.

He turns and carries me through the darkened room, and then we're falling, toppling onto the bed. Luke braces his weight on his elbows, our mouths never losing contact, our tongues refusing to stop the mating duel they're engaged in.

I reach to unbuckle his belt. "Not yet," he growls, reaching for my hands and pinning them above me. "Stay," he commands in a way so much like an Alpha, a moan escapes my lips and neither of us have even removed our pants yet.

He unbuttons my jeans, his eyes searing me as totally as his mouth does as he guides my legs until I'm free. "Beautiful," he whispers, and I feel it.

He crawls back, the predatory grace sending a shiver through me. I gasp when he takes my breast in his mouth, his tongue circling my nipple in the most delightful way. Just when I think I can't wait any longer, when I'm ready for more, he stops. Whimpering, my eyes search his, eliciting a deep laugh that shakes my entire body. The shadows around him are fading and for a brief moment, I think I see the person he was before life stole him away.

My fingers are back in his silky hair, tugging him up, but he growls a refusal. With a trail of kisses from my breasts, to my stomach, and lower still... His tongue teases me as his teeth nip at my undies, making them magically melt away. Eyes glittering with an almost possessive desire, he watches my face as his hand slips between my thighs. My mouth falls open on a silent gasp and my eyes close as his fingers find my folds. He teases the sensitive flesh, then rings the opening that I've barely given much thought to, but is now the center of my universe.

Luke groans. "Fuck you're wet."

My legs instinctively fall open, wanting more of the sharp pleasure. His fingers draw slow circles around my clit, making me arch my back as I cry out. I never knew I was so responsive. That it would be so easy to elicit pleasure. "Luke," I moan, not entirely sure what I'm asking for.

"I'm not going anywhere, gorgeous," he murmurs.

The circling on my clit becomes faster, firmer as he moves back up to kiss me once more. I'm a writhing mass of sensations beneath him as electric passion climbs along every nerve.

Somehow, it starts and converges on that one place where his expert hand is touching me.

Unable to last much longer, I move my hands to his belt, relieved when he doesn't stop me. In fact, he helps, seeming as impatient as I am to have the rest of his clothes off. Once he's also naked, Luke stretches out beside me, quickly resuming the sweet torment between my legs. His hot gaze roams my face, my body, my very soul as if he's trying to brand it all.

Beyond the ability to speak, I reach for his cock and grasp it, finding it far harder and hotter than I expected, and suddenly wondering if I should be gentle. Luke looks at me confused, and I know I must be doing it wrong, but he doesn't say a word. Instead, he wraps his hand around mine, tightening my grasp. I comply, purring with delight when his eyes close, pleasure tightening his handsome features. I move faster, gripping a little more tightly, and I'm rewarded with a small bead of moisture appearing on the tip. Luke groans, biting his lip in a way that has feminine pride coursing through me. Making me bolder. I run my tongue over his jaw, tasting the sweat beading on his throat as my grip tightens and my hand picks up pace

To my surprise, he reaches down and loosens my hand, weaving our fingers together. "I...I can't wait any longer," he gasps.

"Then stop holding back," I whisper, drawing his mouth to mine.

I kiss Luke, showing him exactly what he's done to me. With a ragged groan, he positions himself above me, the tip of his hot cock settling at my entrance. For a brief second, I wonder if I should tell him. Should I warn him I'm a virgin? Will he know? Will it hurt as bad as they say? My body is begging the logical Addy who ensures everything is in place, who follows the rules, to shut the ever-loving hell up and enjoy this moment.

And so I do. I arch and move so he's notched inside me, on the precipice of making me his.

A bead of sweat zig zags down Luke's temple and he looks like he's gritting his teeth. Yet he must know this is my first time because he's far gentler than I could ever imagine someone as strong and gruff as him being. He enters me, inch by excruciating inch, never stopping, but never rushing. In fact, he watches me with an intensity that would take my breath away if I hadn't forgotten to breathe.

There's a slight pinch, and he pauses, possibly noticing, but I'm determined that it won't get in the way. That it's just the old Addy objecting as she's shoved away. I dig my nails into his shoulder, impaling myself on the rest of his length.

"Ah!" Luke groans, arching so that he's completely inside me, the tendons in his throat standing out in sharp relief.

I cry out, blinded with pleasure. The fullness. The touching of places I didn't know exist. The way every nerve ending just came alive. It's overwhelming.

And I want more.

We start moving simultaneously, breaths picking up as the pace does. I rake my nails down his back like some animal as the pleasure quickens. It contracts around the place our bodies are meeting faster and faster, climbing through me. Consuming me. We become a frantic, thrusting, ravenous being of movement.

"Dammit, Addy," Luke gasps as if he's the one acting contrary to his nature and not the other way around. "You're dangerous, you know that?"

Something between a whimper and moan escapes me. "So are you," I whisper.

He leans down to kiss me, his powerful body never once breaking stride, and I kiss him with abandon, the sensations becoming primal. If only he knew the delightful shift that's unraveling beneath him. The old Adeline is being replaced by a new woman, someone I don't recognize but is filled with a power I never experienced before.

And then I'm not unraveling any more. I'm coming together. I'm soaring, cresting, being swept away.

And I'm crying out as pleasure rocks through me.

CHAPTER 3

LUKE

Addy's body quakes beneath mine, my name on her lips far more rousing than any explicit content I've consumed. Watching her come as I pound her pussy is the sexiest, most breath-taking thing I've ever seen.

It propels my own pleasure, and I thrust harder and faster than I ever have. I bite back the one word that keeps climbing up my throat.

Mine.

Instead, I focus on the explosion that's building. It grips me by the spine, tightens my balls, and rips through me before I'm ready. My cock jerks inside of her, ejecting endless hot streams of come into her quivering heat. Ecstasy is like a mushroom cloud through my entire being, shredding reality, making Addy the focal point of my universe. It locks every muscle even as it blazes every thought. Any defenses.

Any sliver of knowledge that I'm losing myself to the enemy.

"Fuck," I moan, my body collapsing, shivering, and reacting in a way I never have before.

Breathing hard, I fall to the side, trying to put some distance between her as aftershocks ripple through me. But Addy follows, wrapping herself around me. She even presses a kiss to my jaw before tucking her head into my shoulder.

I blink up at the roof of the motel room, trying to get my breathing under control. Maybe then any of this will make sense. I'd planned a great deal in advance of what to expect and prepare for when I investigated this rival pack, slowly infiltrating their bar, Moonlit. I played out a lot of possibilities, especially with how I'd make use of Addy, but I definitely didn't bank on having sex right after we officially met. I most certainly didn't count on becoming putty in the hands of a murderer.

She goes to lift her head, but I keep it nestled in my shoulder, even drawing her tighter so she doesn't see it as a rejection. I hate how good it feels when she relaxes against me. How can I be so drawn to someone so evil? How can a murderer like her feel so much like home? What the hell is wrong with me? Not only have I betrayed my family but it'd be a miracle if I even step foot in Moonlit again. Much less welcomed into the pack.

Addy shivers, and I quickly draw up the covers, glad to cover the glory that is her naked body, even as I mourn devouring it with my eyes. How am I going to fix this? One-night stands are not the way to a woman's heart, least of all the way to earn the pack's trust.

Her fingers shift a little on my chest, even that slight movement making my cock twitch. "That was pretty good, huh?" she whispers, sounding almost shy.

As if she didn't just give me the best fucking sex of my life.

Conscious I need to redeem this situation somehow, I allow the truth to be said. "I'd say we surpassed 'pretty good," I admit.

I'm pretty sure I feel her smile. "I agree," she whispers and says no more.

As the seconds stretch out, I half expect her to get up and

leave. Isn't that what a one-night stand is? Fuck 'em and leave 'em? It's exactly what I'd expect from someone from her pack. Instead, she nestles in closer, even looking up. Her eyes search mine, as if she's checking this is okay.

Even though I know I'm playing a dangerous game, in the same way I couldn't slow down the moment I touched her silken skin, I can't seem to push her away. What is wrong with me? I briefly wonder if it's some wolf-thing my parents skimmed over when telling us their version of the birds and the bees...

"Can we just rest a moment?" she yawns before nuzzling into my chest. All logic says I should deny her, says I should feel wretched for what I've done—and I do, kind of—but I can't seem to tell her no. I stroke her hair, and everything melts away as her heartbeat slows. It feels so sweet. So trusting...

Before I can scoff at my own stupidity, my own eyelids become heavy. I fight it for a second—sleep and I don't have a great relationship—but then the warmth of the girl holding me seeps past my skin and straight into my chest. It just feels too good. Almost...comforting.

The shadows follow me there, like they always do, dancing in a circle around my old home, screaming, "They're dead. They're dead. They're dead." I tense, ready to rouse myself, when they do something they've never done before. They fade. Instead, a strange light fills the space, erasing all the darkness from my past and I find myself slipping into a new dream. A dream of Addy's lips and hips and sighs.

I wake up to the sound of my phone's alarm crying out. Addy jolts awake, her eyes wide as if we're about to be attacked. The irony. I suppose when you kill people for the fun of it, you likely make a lot of enemies along the way. Something to consider, I realize. Did I lock my car doors?

"Geez! Your alarm could wake the whole town, including the cemetery!" she says, catching her breath.

I chuckle. "I know," I say and quickly silence my phone's alarm. It's a reminder to take sleeping pills—the ones that are supposed to help with the nightmares. At this point, the irony of tonight would be funny if it wasn't so damn disgusting.

Addy pulls the covers up to her chest as if she's some virgin. "Why do you have alarms at this hour? It's not even morning. I mean, we couldn't have been asleep for more than an hour."

"I like to make sure I'm home at a reasonable hour," I quip, intentionally dodging her question.

"Do you lose track of time in hotels with girls you just met often then?" She blushes, and I can tell she instantly regrets her question. There was no malice in her tone, no assumption, and why should there be? This was nothing but a one-night stand, right? Surely she didn't see this as something more. Not someone so cold and cruel.

Lost in thought, her sad girl eyes bring me back to the present. I haven't even answered her yet. "Sometimes," I murmur, "but never quite like this. I don't usually stick around after..." And I don't usually enjoy it that much, and...it's not usually with someone I'm seeking to punish.

Addy ponders this, picking her next words slowly, carefully. "Well, I'm glad you did. This time."

Strange how my body insists I say "me too" even though I have every reason not to. "It is late, though." Looking at the clock, I can't believe Addy's right that I hadn't even been asleep for an hour—my night with her wasn't only the best sex I've ever had, but it was also the best nap I've had in ages. And I didn't even take my tablets yet!

She bites her lip, as if pleading for another round, and it

takes everything in me to put this to a halt. "I best be going home."

Her teeth release her bottom lip, her tongue licking the corners. "Oh?"

"Yeah," I continue and pluck the most truthful lie I can. "I promised my grams I'd be taking her to the Strawberry Festival in the morning."

"Wait? What?" Addy sits up taller, quickly tucking the covers around her chest. "That's adorable. Oh, I bet she loves the festival! I know I love it. My ma and paps took me every year growing up. They have the best strawberry jam in the whole county, you know? They even were on some fancy food network show and ..." She trails off, and starts laughing. "Sorry, I do that sometimes."

"Do what?" I ask, tilting my head, to which she also matches—a wolf-thing so ingrained in our DNA most of us don't even realize it. I catch myself before it makes me smile.

"You know, just ramble on about stuff that no one cares about." She waves a dismissive hand.

"I like hearing you talk," I say before I can stop myself. I almost curse. My need to wipe away the flash of insecurity on her face had me blurting the truth. I want to know more about this girl.

Because I need to learn about her family, I tell myself grimly.

A sudden spark flashes across her face and without a word, she reaches to snatch my phone. Instinctively I resist, grabbing it first from the bedside table and holding my arm behind my head. Raising an eyebrow, I ask, "And what do you think you're doing?"

She flicks her hair and lifts her chin, any show of confidence undermined by the fact she yanks up the sheets a little higher. "Give me your phone," she commands.

"Now—" I nearly call her out for possessing such Alpha energy, tempted to ask if she can keep up with my own Alpha nature before I remember she can't know who I am. "Miss Addy, why would I do such a thing? If you need me to call you an Uber."

"I don't need a ride. I practically live next door and—" her voice fades out as reality wraps its arms around my throat, stealing the air from my lungs.

My stomach spins as the room goes out of focus. I had sex with a murderer—someone who is responsible for my parent's death, my entire family's death, everything—and I not only liked it, I mean of course its sex, but it was truly the most blissful moment of my life. Sucking in a deep breath, I do my best to ground myself in the current moment...no, not the current moment, that makes the room spin even more ...

It's Addy's voice that pulls me out of the darkness. "What's wrong?" her voice is teasing, an attempt to lighten the tone, "Not used to others barking orders at you?"

I chuckle, acknowledging that's the truth. I don't have a pack thanks to her family. Eager to get out of here and sort out the mess in my head, I hand her my phone. She begins typing away, a wicked smirk on her face. When she hands me back my phone, she says, "You just sent me a text." She picks up her own phone, unlocks it to her text messages, and holds it in front of me.

Thanks for the best night of my life.

I laugh, hoping it doesn't sound strained. What is it about this girl and cutting straight to the truth? "Cute," I say, before grabbing my keys. "Are you sure you don't need an Uber? It's late and dark and—" And she's a killer. Of course, someone as lethal as Addy wouldn't want a ride home. She has nothing to fear in the dark because she is the monster in the shadows.

"No, I think I'm just gonna hang out here a bit longer and

head back... It was good. This." She flushes. "I mean, well, you know what I mean."

"I do." I pause and look her straight in the eye, baffled how she doesn't see the danger she's in. "See you around, Adeline." A silent threat laces around my gruff voice, something Addy clearly mistakes for lust, leaving her to blush in anticipation as I slip out the door.

Outside, I pause. A cool rain falls from the sky as if it can wash away the guilt and the sins of tonight. Gritting my teeth, I look forward to it. I can't drop my guard like that again.

I will not melt under the hand of a woman who killed my family.

No, she will crumple under me.

CHAPTER 4
ADELINE

I'm still shell-shocked when I step out of the motel shower a few minutes later. I towel myself down and quickly get dressed, noting the way my skin still tingles.

Did I just...?

Straightening, I catch my reflection in the mirror across the room. I touch my lips, blinking. I did.

I just had the most amazing experience of my life!

And the soreness between my legs is proof of that. I'd bled a little, which is one of the reasons for the shower. The other is that I now have to go home, pretending as if nothing's changed. I don't know much about sex, being a virgin and all, but I do know one thing—shifters swear they can smell it. One of our more rebellious pack mates, Lindsey, always says to shower, shower again, and then shower some more. So I did, scrubbing with the cheap soap as if my life depended on it.

I find myself smiling, looking a little like a star-struck idiot. Luke's promise to see me sends a thrill through my spine and a bounce in my step as I make my way to the door. I always expected my first time to be a mess or to be fumbling and awkward, but somehow we fell into place, into each other as if this was something we were meant to do. As if we just fit.

And he wants to see me again.

The moment I step out, a light sprinkle of rain falls over me, but it doesn't dampen my spirits. I'm pretty sure I'll be floating for days thanks to the high of my first time. My first time with Luke.

Except I quickly discover I'm not alone. Luke hasn't left like he said he would.

Because my pack-mates are standing in front of him.

The tallest and widest steps forward and my stomach turns to knots. It's my oldest brother, Lawrence, and although I've always shown him the respect that role entails, I also know he's a bully. "I heard you were dancing with my sister," he seethes, glaring at Luke as he stalks closer.

I call out, terrified of what I'm about to watch unfold, but Lawrence ignores me. "We're a big family and we take care of our own, you hear?" A ripple of growls rise from the shifters behind him, lips curling to reveal flashes of white teeth. "If you hurt her, I'm not the only one who will hurt you."

A cold smile curls around the edges of Luke's lips. So incongruent with the man I just made love to. "It's too late for that."

Although I have no idea what that means—Luke's already hurt me, or my pack's already hurt him?—I break into a run. I know the look on Lawrence's face. I've seen it before when he's about to unleash his temper on another of our brothers. He doesn't stop until blood is drawn.

Lawrence grips the cuff of Luke's shirt, slamming him against his truck. "Leave. Her. Alone."

Heart thundering, I jam myself between them. "No. You leave him alone."

Lawrence looks astounded to find me there, pushing against his chest. In fact, I'm pretty sure I hear Luke's startled intake of breath behind me. Honestly, I can't quite believe I'm standing here myself.

I just can't let Luke get hurt because of my choices.

"I don't want any trouble," I say to Lawrence, lowering my voice. "We didn't do anything wrong."

And that part is the truth. My time with Luke could only be described as one thing—right.

Lawrence hesitates, and I drop my voice even more. "Remember who we are."

We can't afford to be seen attacking a lone human. It would bring too much attention to the pack.

My brother steps back, baring his teeth. "If we see you around again..." he threatens.

Luke doesn't respond as I feel him turn around, then hear his truck door opening. Once Lawrence has retreated a few steps, I move away, also turning so I can have one last glance at Luke. I want to apologize that our night ended like this.

Any words freeze in my throat.

Luke's green eyes are glacial. His face is a mask of anger. And he's looking right at me.

My hand flutters to my throat as I try to reconcile our heated moments with the cold anger I'm now faced with. Something flashes across his face—regret? Anguish? Hatred?—before he snaps his head back to the windshield.

Without another look, he roars away in a squeal of tires.

I tiptoe my way across the lawn, mentally preparing for my parents and their shifter-hearing to pick up the pit-pat-pit-pat of each step. I may have talked Lawrence down, and he was drunk enough that I'm hoping he might actually forget he had that run-in with Luke, but my parents won't be so easily convinced. They'll be sober. And they've tried to ensure something like this would never happen.

They'll never see the irony that their overprotectiveness is what had me sneaking out in the first place.

Lost in thought between quietly taking my next step and promising myself that the last glance from Luke was my imagination, I don't notice a figure standing in front of me until I bump into it. I gasp, already filled with panic and stumbling over my explanation as to why I'm coming home so late.

Before I can get a word out the figure hushes me and I finally realize it's not my parents. "Lindsey!" I breathe a sigh of relief and nearly collapse in her arms.

"Hiding from the fam?" She winks mischievously. "Don't worry. They were calling around to figure out why you didn't come home. We had an amazing slumber party, by the way, full of cheesy nineties movies and your favorite moose track ice cream."

"My favorite ice cream is cookie dough." I shake my head, processing that Lindsey covered for me. Did my parents buy it? Well, they must've if she's here. "Thank you?"

"You can thank me by telling me what juicy things you've been up to. Here," she grabs my hand, lacing her fingers in mine, "let's go to my place."

Glad for the reprieve, I allow her to tug me along. Lindsey's one of the few pack members who has her own place without any family or other pack members. Her parents died when she was young and though the pack tried finding her a mate and she had plenty of suitors, she never quite fit the role of an obedient girl. If it wasn't for the dead parents card, she'd be sent off the compound, I'm sure. They go easy on Lindsey, despite her rebellious nature. A lot easier than they would ever go on me.

It's about a ten-minute walk to get to Lindsey's cabin from

here, and it's even longer when taking a more secluded path. We both remain quiet—aware that a few of the shifters like to roam in the early mornings. We take a collective deep breath as we reach her cabin, her fingers unlacing from mine, and I realize she was just as scared as I was. I never thought Lindsey was scared of anything, but lying to an Alpha is risky for any shifter.

She locks the door behind us and makes sure all her curtains are closed. I'm surprised to see a pile of nineties movies, popcorn, wine, and yes, an empty container of moose track ice cream, sitting on a pile of blankets on the floor.

She winks. "I'm a good liar."

Coffee wafts through the air and I gratefully watch as Lindsey pours us both a cup. Taking a seat next to her at the kitchen table, I know I'm going to have to tell her something, because unlike her, I'm not a good liar.

"Spill," she commands.

"Well," I say, deciding to go with the truth, "I was at Moonlit last night." That alone is enough to cause her jaw to drop.

"Addy! You didn't? Wait—was that your first time?"

Blushing, I begin to nod, and immediately realize she means my first time at the bar. "No," I correct myself. "Not really. I've gone in a few times. Just to get out, you know? But there is this guy and we, well, we went to a motel..."

"Adeline, do you mean to tell me you hooked up with this 'guy'?"

I nod, surprised a flush doesn't crawl up my neck.

Lindsey leans forward, eyes alight with curiosity. "How much did you hook up? I know you said you went to a motel, but did you... Did you two...you know?"

"Have sex?" I say boldly. "It's not a dirty word, Linds. Yes, I had sex and it just so happened to be glorious."

She nearly spits out her coffee. "Okay, who are you and what did you do with sweet little Addy who can barely hold her head high when asked her name?"

I giggle. "I don't know, actually, I just felt like I wanted to be different. More like you, in a way. I am always on such a short leash and heck, I guess I just wanted to have some fun."

"He was your first time," she notes, putting together the pieces as she taps her lips with her fingertips. "How long have you two been seeing each other? That must've been hard to hide from everyone."

"We haven't," I admit.

"You absolute dog, Addy! Are you truly telling me you had a one-night stand with—wait, is this person even in our pack?"

I shake my head. "He's not one of us."

Looking stunned, Lindsey sips her coffee, and I realize I've neglected mine. I grab the honey and cream she placed beside me and fill the cup, stirring it around until she says something. Except it seems I've silenced her.

"So?" I whisper, sipping my coffee, looking up at her over the steam.

"So..." she pauses, a wicked smile playing across her lips. "Tell me everything!"

And so I do. We move to the living room, and as a nineties movie plays in the background—so I have one less lie to tell my parents—I spill every last detail. I tell her about his hot green eyes. The way he couldn't seem to keep his hands off me. The way I loved every second of it.

Somewhere in the middle, we end up wrapped in blankets, eating freshly popped popcorn, acting just the way two women would during a girl's night. Giggling and reliving what's fast become the best night of my life, I even tell Lindsey about Lawrence. She assures me she's had entire conversations with my brother when he's drunk, and he's had no recollection of it the following day.

For a moment, the image of Luke's furious face before he drove off rises in my mind, but I push it away. He can't have looked like that at me after what we shared. It's impossible for those two emotions to coexist even within the same state.

"When he left, he promised he'd see me around," I swoon, but a knowing look in Lindsey's eyes has me stopping. I bite my lip, deciding not to defend myself.

Sure, I know that men whisper all kinds of promises to get in a girl's pants, but this was different. Luke was different. I try to tell Lindsey as much but she's already turning down the TV volume and yawning as she gestures to the clock. I nod, acknowledging we both definitely need some sleep. She slinks off to her room, while I try to make myself comfortable on the couch.

I open up my phone, smiling at the goofy text I sent from Luke's phone to mine. I didn't get a chance to apologize for my brother's behavior and while I know I shouldn't text him so soon, and if anything maybe I should let him text me first, I can't just not apologize. I keep it short and simple, and the moment I hit send my heart starts fluttering again.

When I finally do fall asleep, I swear I can feel Luke's arms wrapped around me. As if his spirit is holding me still.

CHAPTER 5
LUKE

*S*creams *fill the air. I run for my life, but they grow louder, reaching toward me and trying to consume every fiber of my being, trying to claw their way out of the bloodbath they're being swallowed by.*

I wake with a start, realizing I'd been dreaming. I sit forward, jamming my hands in my hair. The nightmares are back, reminding me it's impossible to forget the night I lost my family.

When I glance at the alarm clock on my bedside drawer, it reads five am. A few hours ago, I was in bed with the enemy. Adeline. The thought of her washes over me, banishing the memories of my dying family from my mind. It's surprising how I want to think about her. Her own family ruined my life, robbing me of everything good that exists. But somehow, Adeline got me in bed with her. As much as I feel uncomfortable remembering myself fucking her till she gasped my name, I close my eyes and embrace the memory, wishing it hadn't come to an end.

Then her brother's snarling face crawls into my mind. Adeline called him Lawrence. His warning had been simple and clear. Not that I'm planning to listen to the wolf and stay away from his sister, but I have to admit that his confrontation unnerved me a little. Staring into Lawrence's unwelcoming face and sensing his barely leashed violence, I knew I need to be careful around these people. Including Adeline. My lust for her can't cloud my reasoning. Her family is dangerous, and any misstep on my part will end any possibility of justice

When the fuck did you start caring about a woman you had a one-night stand with, Luke? I ask myself as I get out of bed, walking into my bathroom. I turn on the tap, scoop some water and splash it on my face. The cold soothes my skin and I splash more on my face. I grab my towel, looking back at myself in the mirror. These eyes that have seen pain. This face that's the reflection of disaster.

My phone buzzes on the bedside drawer where I'd placed it last night. When I go back to my room and check the screen, I see that it is a call from Adeline. Her number isn't saved on my phone but I learned the last digits of her phone number from the text she sent me. I don't want to talk to her. Not yet.

I need to get myself back under control first.

The phone beeps and Adeline's name vanishes from the phone's screen. My thumb lingers on the dial button, tempting me to return the call and hear her voice again. Her moans from last night slither into my thoughts again, tightening my crotch. I want to hear her call my name again. I want to hear Adeline scream my name until she collapses in my arms, overwhelmed by what exploded between us last night.

I am about to toss my phone to the bed when a text message comes in.

Hey, Luke. I want to apologize for my brother's behavior yester-day. He's always been protective of me.

There's a pause, and another text arrives.

I want to make it up to you. I know a friend who is one of the

organizers of the Strawberry Festival and I can get you and your grandmother front row tickets. Just text me back if you're up to it.

Although the text message is light and friendly, my cock is already hard. It's certainly up for it. My hand tightens around the cell phone. My cock is the issue. Especially when it thinks it's connected to my heart. My lips flatline. It's a good thing Addy's found a man who's triggered her fascination and made her come last night. It's a fucking great thing it's me.

Especially when the thought it could be someone else jolts green fire through my veins.

I push away the thoughts. Adeline's desire to have me in bed with her again is exactly what I planned. Having to go to a festival with a grandmother I don't have is the actual issue. I only came up with the lie so she'd think I'm living a normal life.

"Shit!" I exclaim, remembering there is more I have to do to make sure Adeline remains ignorant of my lies. Especially when I need that second date.

Where the hell am I going to find a grandmother? Who would be willing to pretend to be an old woman and consistently lie to a lady who just wants to get into my pants a second time?

I scroll through the contacts on my phone and find a number. It is the only person who's capable of pulling me out of this mess. The call picks up on the third ring.

"Oh, there you are! You haven't called me in days," her high-pitched voice says over the phone.

"Sorry, Jacqueline. I've been busy," I tell her.

Honestly, I feel guilty about not calling her or checking up on her. Jacqueline Jones took me in after my pack got slaughtered. I owe her enough to care about her, even though I'm no longer living with her. In fact, she didn't want me to leave, but my unrepentant wish to make Adeline's family pay was enough to pull me away from Jacqueline. I don't want her caught up in the ugly aftermath of my vengeance. She deserves better than that.

"Busy? Are you avoiding me, Luke?"

I chuckle and sit on my bed. "Is that even possible? No, I'm not avoiding you, Jacqueline. I just have a lot of things on my plate right now."

"Does that include preparations for my birthday?"

I facepalm. Damn! Jacqueline's birthday is this month and I'd completely forgotten about it.

"Yes," I lie. "It includes preparations for your birthday. What do you want this year?"

Jacqueline doesn't reply immediately. I can hear her humming over the phone, an indication that she's thinking about an answer. This is the woman I'm about to beg to pretend to be my grandmother? Jacqueline is in her fifties but she loves behaving like a teenager. She inputs emojis in her texts, uses slang she thinks is still current and isn't fully dressed without studs in her nose and rings on her fingers.

"I'll think about it and text you," she finally replies. "But you have to get me whatever I tell you I want. You didn't get me anything last year."

Actually, Jacqueline didn't celebrate her birthday last year. She'd gone through a horrible break-up on the morning of her birthday and I didn't buy her anything because she kept crying all day. Jacqueline's been single all her life and the only man, Mark Slater, whom she thought was the right person for her turned out to be an absolute douchebag. Love does nothing but wreck a person. It weakens them and turns them into a shadow of themselves.

"Sure," I respond. "I'll get you anything you want as long as it is not above my paycheck."

Jacqueline laughs. "You work in a bar, Luke. I'm not going to ask you to buy me a Ferrari. Although, telling Mark to go fuck himself while I drive past him in one sounds like a good idea."

"There will be no Ferrari and there will be no telling Mark that. Forget about him, Jacqueline."

"I can't," Jacqueline says and I note the pain in her voice. "I still think about him."

Right now, I feel like racing to her apartment and hugging her. She's a total trainwreck and the endless insults I hurl at Mark just to make her feel good rarely works. She loves him and I hate that she's given in to the soul-consuming illusion of love.

I don't know what it means to love. In my former pack, we were trained to respect the pack's blood ties and nothing more. Back then, I had a list of annoying wolves I would have very much loved to rip out their throats but it would be treason to kill another wolf without cause. Also, when I found my mate, the discovery wasn't founded on love. Every wolf is born to find a mate. I had found mine but she got taken away from me before I could even completely take her as mine.

"I have to go now," Jacqueline's voice pulls me out of my reverie. "Do stop by my apartment this weekend. I miss seeing that cute face of yours."

"Don't go yet," I quickly say. "I need your help."

"Ha! I knew it. You called me for a reason."

"I'm sorry, Jacqueline. But this is important."

"It's okay." Her laughter bubbles through. "I'm not angry. You can always call me whenever you need my help. That was what I told you the day you moved out, right?"

"Yes," I answer and draw in a breath. "This will sound weird but I need you to pretend you're my grandmother."

A long silence. I picture Jacqueline's face morphing into a look of disbelief while a smile of mockery stretches across her lips.

"You're joking, right?" Jacqueline asks. She's trying hard not to laugh.

"I'm not. Look, there is this girl I met..."

"There's a girl?" Jacqueline shrieks. "Why didn't you start with that?"

"Just a girl, Jacqueline. She's not important but I lied to her yesterday that I have a grandmother and I'm taking her to the Strawberry Festival. She texted me this morning that..."

"You have her number?" Jacqueline interrupts me again, her voice going a range higher.

"This will be a whole lot quicker if you stop interrupting me," I say, exasperated.

"Sorry." She clears her throat. "Continue."

I wait for a few seconds, expecting her to say something again. She doesn't. So, I continue, "She is going to be at the Festival, and I don't have a grandmother. Will you be my grandmother for a few hours?"

"Oh, dear, Luke," Jacqueline tells me. "I spend hours every morning removing the strands of gray hair on my head. Then they grow back because life keeps mocking me that growing old is an inevitable journey in my life. I hate being old."

"I know. I get it." I rub my forehead, wondering who else I can call in my lone wolf world.

"Hmm. If this girl isn't important, just don't go to the Festival. Something came up. You can't show up. She can go fuck herself."

Well, I have fucked Adeline and I want to do it again. A lot.

Shaking my head, I repress a sigh at my wayward thoughts. "It's not that easy."

"It is. Go to work and come home after that. Stay in bed and binge-watch Netflix. There's this new show about fallen angels who—"

"Jacqueline!" I growl.

I don't mean to but Jacqueline doesn't understand how important getting close to Adeline is. I need to infiltrate her pack and slaughter the murderers who killed my family.

"She is important, yeah?" she asks, as intuitive as ever, even if she doesn't know why.

I take a deep breath. "Yes, she is."

"Great. I wanted to hear you say that. Fine, I'll come with you to the Festival. Gosh! I have to hire an old woman's outfit so I can smell like one. Actually, old Mrs. Patty downstairs won't mind helping with that. She smells of cats. I'll have to smell of cats."

I break into a smile. "Thank you, Jacqueline."

CHAPTER 6

ADELINE

I wake slowly, not willing to relinquish the hold on sleep. Those are the hours where my dreams are full of a man fucking me until I'm quivering with pleasure. A man who watches you with hot eyes as you climb, then flares with satisfaction when you tumble right over the precipice. Every moment is divine and I don't want to leave.

But being a member of my pack means everything good always comes to an end. I fling my eyes open as the first sound of someone racing down the corridor clatters through my room. Something thuds to the ground and I hear one of my brothers yell. "Twenty seconds! Woot! Lawrence smashes it again!"

I jump out of bed and storm out of my room, missing a collision with Lawrence's husky wolf body by a hairbreadth. I snarl at him as he halts and turns around to face me.

"Will you stop with the noise?" I cry.

My brother morphs into his human form as he approaches me. His fur vanishes while his muscled body narrows into a less intimidating one. He stares at me, a derisive smile crawling up his lips.

"Look who's awake," he sneers.

"I just want to sleep. Is that too much to ask?" I ask, throwing my hands out wide. I want to be lost in my dreams of Luke.

Lawrence sighs and brushes a strand of hair from my face. "It's fine, sister. I'm just training. How was your night?"

I look at him like he had just sprouted two horns from his head—though, I won't be surprised if that happens. Lawrence has never asked me about my night.

"Uh, fine."

Lawrence wags a finger at me. "That's not what I heard."

His words hit me like a violent wave. Lawrence was deeply drunk last night. I'd assumed he wouldn't remember confronting Luke. But if Jake told him, or if he remembers, I'm scared of what he'll do to me. He hates seeing me with guys.

"I rang Lindsey this morning," Lawrence is saying and I have to stop my hand from flying to my mouth. I hadn't expected her to betray me. "She said you ate every last spoonful of her moose track ice cream."

Relief washes over me. Lawrence is still the pathetic drunk he is. If he'd stripped himself naked and danced in front of the whole world yesterday, he still wouldn't remember a thing.

"Maybe." I turn back to my door. "Can you just train quietly, please?"

Lawrence's body rakes with laughter. "It's impossible, Addy. You know I have to train my wolf form to be faster and stronger. We don't know what enemies are out there, lurking."

I cross my arm. "Isn't High Ridge Pack the safest pack in the area? Why are you bothered about enemies?"

Lawrence doesn't look me in the eye when he answers, "Just go back to sleep. I'll train outside."

I know when my brother is lying. He's keeping something from me but I don't pressure him to tell me. To be fair, I'm hiding something from him too. Luke.

"It's too late now," I huff, those moments with Luke now nothing but a memory. I turn back to my room. "Like you care, anyway," I mutter.

Damian, my other brother who's keeping records of Lawrence's sprints, frowns, "Enough of the drama, Addy. If you want to go back into your room, do so and stop whining."

I roll my eyes and go back into my room. Lawrence and Damian appear to love giving me a hard time. I wish Jake was out there with them. He always backs me up.

My brothers don't involve me in all they do and I've come to live with it. The Pack has its way of subjugating the female wolves and sidelining them when it comes to important issues. I stay in my room for hours, trying to finish up the latest romance novel Lindsey bought me some days ago. Sometimes, I hear the howls of my brothers outside the walls of the mansion we call home and I stop to watch them train in the woods with others in our pack.

Even then, the hours crawl slowly. In the end, I'm proud that I don't start to get ready until an hour before the Strawberry Festival. I refuse to be some silly teen who spends hours on what to wear or flustering over her makeup.

Still, I hurry into the bathroom and scrub myself clean. I spend extra minutes brushing my hair to a gloss. I spin one way, then the other in the mirror, appraising my snug jeans and top with tiny strawberries printed on it.

Rolling my eyes at the flush in my cheeks, I grab my cross bag and sneak out of my room. My brothers are still in the woods. By the time they get back, they'll find me gone. I don't want to tell them where I'm headed. Lawrence and Damian will ask unending questions and probably lock me up in my room if I don't provide satisfactory answers.

As I get to the ground floor of the mansion, I notice that the front door is slightly ajar. I freeze, wondering if one of my brothers came back without my knowledge. I've been watching them all day!

I approach the door and stretch a hand to grab the knob. A loud crashing noise comes from the kitchen and I spin around in time to see Damian glaring at me from the doorway.

"Dammit, Damian!" I yell, placing a hand on my chest.

He's tearing into a piece of raw meat while he looks at me. Beef! The smell of the dead animal wafts into my nostrils, awakening my subdued hunger. I'd deliberately gone hungry because I didn't want to fill my stomach and not eat strawberries at the Festival.

"Where are you going?" Damian asks, chewing the meat sloppily.

"Uh, out? Where else will I be going?" I tell him, trying to hide my nervous tone.

"Where are you going?" Damian repeats. This time, his voice is deep and I know he's on the verge of ranting at me.

"The library," I quickly respond.

Damian eyes me. He throws the last of the meat into his mouth and walks towards me. I lock my gaze on him, pretending to not be scared. But Damian is the craziest of my brothers. He blindly follows Lawrence's orders and hell hath no madness like a follower with no mind of his own.

"What?" I say, desperately working on evening out my breathing.

His next action surprises me. Damian inches his face closer to mine and begins to sniff me. His grating voice send chills down my spine as he says, "I can smell that stranger on you. It's faint because you did a lot of scrubbing but you know I pick up even the faintest scents. What's his name again?"

I swallow hard. "Are you talking about Luke?"

"Yes, Luke."

"We talked at the bar. That's why you can smell him on me."

Damian chuckles. "Oh, please, I wasn't born yesterday." He moves his face away from me and adds, "Whatever you did with him last night had better stay in whatever room you did it. We don't welcome strangers here."

I nod. "I know. It's a one time thing," I lie without blinking.

"Good. Or else." Damian bares his fangs at me. "I rip his lungs out."

I grab the doorknob and begin to slide out of the house. "Noted, Damian."

I hurry away from the mansion, not looking behind me as I try to shake off the ice forming in my veins. Damian is on to me but I'm not going to let him get into my head.

Today will be about Luke and no one else.

T he annual Strawberry Festival is known for two things—the crowd of feastful people and the unending display of strawberries.

As I walk through the throngs of lively people clad in decorative clothes capturing every shade of strawberry and embrace the energetic atmosphere, I break into a delighted smile. I'm going to enjoy being here today.

To top it all, Luke's text came in as soon as I stepped into the Festival. He's somewhere here, waiting for me to find him. I glance around the place, looking out for a man who takes my breath away with little more than a glance, even as I try to slow my steps. I don't want Luke to know he's been on my mind since the very second we met yesterday. He's better off not being aware of my obsession.

"How is a beautiful lady like you lost in a place like this?" a familiar voice says behind me.

I wheel around to stare into Luke's intense green eyes. Just like last night, the world melts away. It's just me and him. And the electricity that crackles between us. He smiles at me, flashing me those pearly white teeth of his and I have to stop myself from touching him.

"I was hoping some gorgeous man would find me and help me around this unfamiliar place," I say to him, my hand fluttering to my hair.

Luke chuckles this time. He takes my hand and presses his lips into the back of it. "You look amazing."

A shiver races up my body. I close my eyes and welcome the pleasant sensation his touch builds inside me. It chases away the lingering cold in my veins. He's my invigorating summer in the heart of a sinister fog. My pack is the sinister fog.

"Or else, I'll rip his lungs out." Damian's hostile words slip into my mind against my will. I hate that my brother threatened to kill the man I can't stop thinking about. If only Damian took a moment to learn how amazing Luke is.

"Open your eyes," Luke whispers into my ear.

The scent of his cologne has my head spinning. When I take Luke in, he's leaning close to me and his sexy lips are barely an inch from mine. The memory of how they felt is like an ache in my loins.

He brushes his lips against mine and pulls away. "I want you to meet my grandmother," Luke adds.

I almost pout. Of course he had to start a fire and then douse it. My insides are burning with a sheer need to ask him to make love to me again. The Festival ought to have a restroom. We could always slip into it and cling to each other while we undress as fast as we can, our mouths hungrily ravaging the other. Luke would then turn me around and fuck me from behind as I tried to keep quiet.

"Oh," I answer, banishing the steamy image out of my head. "Where is she?"

"Over there," Luke responds.

He points to his left where a slim woman is talking to another person. As though she knows we're now looking at her, Luke's grandmother glances our way and waves at us. She and Luke share no similar facial looks. While Luke's eyes are guarded and intense, his grandmother's eyes are a temple of unfiltered warmth. The twinkles bear traces of sweet acceptance, as though she's telling me, without saying a word, that she'll always be there for me. Her hair is fully gray but I'm amazed that the wrinkles on her face are few. How old is she?

"Come talk to her." Luke holds my hand and leads me towards his grandmother. "Her name is Jacqueline."

I wear a smile on my face and let Luke take me to the woman. She whispers something to the other woman she'd been talking to. The woman walks away while Jacqueline turns to face us and beams.

"Adeline, is it?" she says. "Oh, you look more beautiful than he described you."

Luke already told his grandmother about me? I don't know why but this melts my heart. It's as though I've been called Luke's wife. *Stop it, Addy! You just met this guy yesterday!*

"Hello, Jacqueline," I answer. "It's great meeting you."

"Me too."

Jacqueline's warm hug is unexpected. She holds me and when I draw a breath, a tiny ball of cat's fur makes for my nose.

I quickly break the hug and say to Jacqueline, "So, do you come to the festival every year?"

"Not every year but I like coming here. I mean, who the hell hates the idea of being surrounded by endless strawberries?"

I laugh. "That's true."

"Jacqueline," Luke says, and I note he doesn't call her Gran or Nana. "Let's pick out some jams and wines. You still want them, don't you?"

"Yeah, I do," Jacqueline answers. She looks at me for a while and then faces Luke. "You know what, son? Forget about picking out the jams and wines. I'll do that myself. Why don't I leave you to hang out with Adeline here?" She pats his arm affectionately. "Do have fun."

Before I can object to her statement because I feel guilty that I'm stopping Luke from picking out jams and wines for his grandma, Jacqueline walks away, calling out to the woman she had been talking to.

Luke faces me. "Looks like it's only the two of us."

My cheeks flush as a gazillion other sexy scenes flit through my mind. "What do you want to do?"

Luke doesn't hesitate before responding, "Why don't we go on the Ferris Wheel?"

CHAPTER 7
LUKE

The last time I ever rode a Ferris Wheel was after my mother's death. My brothers and I had been heart-broken by her loss and my father had let us sneak into the human world to join in a Halloween celebration.

Humans celebrate virtually everything. They spend days preparing for the celebration of the birth of a man who later died on the cross for their sins. Then they wear scary costumes in October and celebrate the Celtic Festival now called Halloween. This afternoon is about Strawberries. The humans happily move around in their strawberry-patterned or straw-berry-colored dresses. It probably means more to them but I don't have time to ask what it is.

I'm here for Adeline. I suppress a frown. I'm here to exact revenge.

The Ferris Wheel jerks under us as it begins to roll. It trans-ports us to the sky and when I think I'm on top of the world, it makes for the ground. I almost bark a laugh. The Ferris Wheel is a total representation of my life. When I felt complete and on top of the world, surrounded by family and friends, disaster took me down, destroying everything like it meant nothing.

"I like the view," Adeline says, staring at the ground where people are small pinkish figures.

The Ferris Wheel takes us up again as I stare at Adeline without her knowing. The wind ruffles her dark hair and the afternoon sunlight caresses her beautiful face. The urge to kiss her, right here, right now, is overwhelming. And she has no idea what she is doing to me.

"Luke?" she says my name, now staring at my face.

I snap out of my thoughts and smile. "Yeah, the view is good."

"What were you thinking about?" Adeline asks, giggling.

"You," I tell her the truth.

I'm not sure of what I see in her eyes but it looks like a glint of excitement. She quickly hides it by lowering her eyes. "Me?"

I watch her carefully as I speak. "I can't really understand what it is about you." My eyes narrow. "You're...special."

Adeline lets out a soft laugh. She looks at me. "Maybe I am."

I let the truth tumble out because it's exactly what any guy on a date would say. Because it brings me closer to my goal. "You fascinate me and I want to know more about you."

"You already know something about me," Adeline replies, her eyes smiling in a way that trips my breath.

"What's that?"

"I have three brothers and one is an unrepentant drunk."

I laugh at her statement, remembering my confrontation with Lawrence. Does she know Lawrence is far more than that? He's a murdered. Just like the rest of her family. I realize I want to picture Adeline as an innocent and ignorant wolf, clueless to the truth. Innocent of the blood they have on their hands.

I pull back imperceptibly. I'd be stupid to think that. What if Adeline's a distraction set up by her brothers? What if Lawrence is out to capture me when I least expect, finally tearing me to pieces in front of his ravenous pack?

The last member of my pack would be dead. Justice would never be served.

"I'm sorry about what he did," Adeline apologizes, reaching over to rest her hand on mine as if she can sense me withdrawing.

I shake my head, trying to clear it of the confusing thought. "I know it's not your fault."

"My family is that way. They're weird."

They're killers! "Why are you doing this?"

Adeline knits her eyebrows together, giving me a confused look. "Doing what?"

"You don't know me," I say, trying not to sound accusing. Or is that desperate? "You just met me last night. I'm a total stranger but it didn't stop you from getting front row tickets for my grandma and me. Why are you being nice to me?"

I expect her to talk about the sex. It has to be the only reason she's trying hard to make friends with me.

"I feel a connection to you," Adeline says softly. "I can't explain it but I just feel it. And no one deserves my brother's treatment. So the front row ticket is my little way of saying sorry."

I stare at her for a long time. Did she just say connection? Does she feel it too?

Fuck. Or is she better at this than I gave her credit for? Is she sucking me in with a false show of vulnerability?

"But despite it all, I love them," Adeline adds, finally glancing up.

My gut clenches as it feels like ice water just flushed through my veins. "Your brothers?"

She nods. "Yes. I love my family. We all look out for each other."

"I see." This is just the reminder I needed.

Adeline looks out at the expansive view as the Ferris Wheel

peaks. "But at the same time, I feel controlled." She returns her gaze to me as she chews her lip. "You know that feeling of being locked up in a cage? You get everything you want. You see everything you want. But you can't spread your wings and fly. You can't feel the wind in your hair. That's what I feel, Luke. I want to break out of my cage and be free."

A tear glistens in her eye. I reach forward and brush it off with my thumb, the need to make the sadness tugging at her features go away clutching my heart. At this moment, I know it's impossible to say no to what's coming. It would be like trying to stop the tide.

My lips touch hers, pulling at the softness and savoring it as though they're the sweetest thing in the world. Adeline moans in my mouth. Her hands move to my back, those long fingers of hers dipping into my skin. She grabs me with the full strength of what she really is—a female wolf in a human world who's pretending to be like the rest.

Adeline doesn't know I'm exactly what she is hiding from me. She doesn't know I can sense the connection between us now, gripping my beating heart with force and quietly telling me she's what I've been looking for. This wolf is mine.

"Sorry," I say as soon as I break the kiss.

I don't want to stop but I'm beginning to hate the secrets we bear. Adeline will never tell me the truth about her family because shifters aren't meant to be known to humans. I can't tell her that I am a wolf too because she would want to find out about my pack. That I don't have a pack, thanks to her family.

I yank back, breathing hard. I'm getting sucked into a whirlpool. Worse, I want to be.

"Is something wrong?" Adeline asks, her cheeks flushed.

"No," I answer quickly. "I'm starting to get tired of the Ferris Wheel."

Adeline peers at the ground again. It's coming closer and the Ferris Wheel seems to be crawling to a stop. "I think it's stopping."

"Let's get out of here."

We get down from the Ferris Wheel and find Jacqueline picking out some jams with her friend. I don't even know the elderly woman's name. Jacqueline deliberately struck up a conversation with an old person to make her age look believable. It's surprising that Jacqueline is still talking to the woman considering this is a friendship based on pretense.

"You're back," Jacqueline says to us as we get to her.

"And you're still picking jams," I respond, eyeing the big jar she has in her hand.

Jacqueline isn't a fan of jams but she got the idea from a short article she read online that old people like them. I don't want her buying things she'll end up emptying into her waste bin. The deal was to check them out and pretend to be interested in buying. However, Jacqueline now has a basket in her hand with two jams in it and she's planning to buy a third one! A bigger one!

"Oh my God!" Adeline mutters beside me.

I look at her and notice she is staring at her wristwatch. When she looks up at me, her flushed face is gone, replaced by eyes darkened with worry.

"What's wrong?"

"I have to get back home," she says, looking a little frantic. "I lied to my brothers that I was going to the library and it's almost two hours since I left. They're going to come looking for me there."

I shake my head. She really takes this little sister act seriously. "You can't be serious. It's just two hours, Addy."

Adeline smiles. I see her cute pink lips curving and the light from her smile reaching up to her eyes. "It's cute when you call me Addy." Except then she pulls back a little farther. "But I'm serious. My brothers are that protective of me. They rarely let me out of their sight."

I realize she's telling the truth. Adeline is scared of her brothers. I know because although my relationship with my father wasn't a toxic one, he carried a power that refused to be challenged. You respected him and his wishes, no matter what.

"Okay. I'll walk you to the bus station."

"You don't have to do that," Adeline says. "I'll find my way home."

It is a subtle way of telling me I'm not welcome to find out who she is. She probably thinks I'll hate the truth—a breathtaking lady like her turning out to be a wolf who changes form and howls at night. *We're the same, Adeline.*

I'm just a broken wolf seeking vengeance for the people who mattered to me.

"Alright." I don't push further. "Thanks for today, Adeline. Though we didn't get to use the front row tickets."

Adeline's eyes are dull with disappointment. She squeezes my hand and says, "Believe me, I wish I could stay."

I peer into the pool of her gorgeous eyes, holding the heated gaze like I want her to remember this very moment. She stares back at me and when I bring my lips close to her ear, a shiver runs through her. The realization that she's again shivering at my touch delights me.

"I want to see you again."

It's the truth, and why I want this so desperately is starting to feel blurred.

She doesn't respond until I've led her outside the arena. "What's your address?" She flushes shyly. "That's if you don't mind me showing up."

What's the harm in telling her where I live? She doesn't

know who I am and seeing my jam-packed one-room apartment would convince her that I'm a human.

And the thought of her in my bed instantly gives me a hard on, flashes of our first night together feeling like flickering flames. There's so much more of her I want to explore. Taste. Devour.

My voice is husky when I respond. "I don't mind."

B y the time I walk into my apartment, the sun's already crawling behind the clouds and I know it's another lonely night for me.

There are times I hunt at night, for wild animals or fresh meat in slaughterhouses. I know a particular butcher, Dave, who'd been employed to feed my family. After my pack was wasted by the High Ridge Pack, he ran out of business. I still remember the shock on his face when I walked into his abattoir weeks after the death of my family.

"No one could have survived that bloodshed," was the first thing he said to me. Dave had seen the massacre. He had been there to deliver meat, only to see the torn bodies of helpless shifters and a realization that all was lost.

"I'll make this right," I'd said to him. "I promise you."

Five years later, I'm no closer to that goal. First, I'm yet to murder the shifters who killed my family. Second, the High Ridge Pack is insanely impenetrable.

And to top it all, I'm currently falling for the enemy.

I sit on my bed and hang my head. It is impossible to deny what Adeline is doing to me. Right now, I miss her. It's not even up to twenty-four hours after meeting her and I want her in my arms again.

She's the very light that can banish the darkness in my

heart. She jolts my static heart to life, as if I've been pulled out of a long term coma and her sublime face is the first I see. Filled with warmth. Pouring into the depth of my cold soul.

"She makes you happy. I can see it on your face," Jacqueline had said to me in the car as I drove her to her apartment.

She'd done a great job pretending to be my grandmother but her pretense was also an avenue to ask me questions about Adeline. The conversation couldn't be avoided.

"Yeah, she's cool," I mumbled.

"She's a very nice girl too," Jacqueline continued, looking out the window. "I wish I could attract nice people."

"Don't say that."

"Whatever." Jacqueline blew air out of her mouth. "You know you'll have to be honest with her about your family. You'll have to tell her the truth."

I didn't look at her as I replied. "I will."

Now, it scares me that there is no escaping the truth. I've begun to develop feelings for Adeline and, one way or the other, I'll have to tell her about what her family had done to me.

After I take a long shower, thinking about the beautiful female shifter who has now taken possession of my mind, I decide to surf the net on my laptop. It's surprising the amount of information you can find on the internet, even information privy to a werewolf.

Just two weeks ago, I created a Facebook profile where I stumbled upon an account dedicated to the idolization of werewolves. I was amused by how much humans love to spread the belief that shifters existed and should be worshiped.

Quite ironic that werewolves are trained to be wary of humans when, in reality, a werewolf's greatest enemy is another werewolf.

I re-read everything I have on the High Ridge Pack. The

family owns most of the vast lands in the northern part of the city and controls several institutions that had once been headed by other packs.

One of them is the Alchemy Institution which had been created by the South Creek Pack to treat wounded or diseased wolves. The High Ridge Pack took control of it five years ago, around the same time they killed my family.

My pack wasn't the only pack they annihilated. These people are looters, taking everything in their path and making it theirs.

The familiar fury burns through my veins. How much does Adeline know about this? And if she doesn't, what will she do when she finds out...

A notification pops up on my screen. It is a message from a texter named Grindelvi. *Hello Luke H., do you want to play the Game of the Night?*

I stare at the screen of my laptop for a while. Game of the Night? It sounds familiar, almost as though I had heard it somewhere before. Another message comes in again. *You can play the Night Wolf and I'll play the Lost Princess.*

Then it hits me.

The Game of the Night is a popular game my father told me about while he was alive. It is the story of a rejected wolf called the Night Wolf who was hated by humans. After their princess goes missing, the Night Wolf finds her lost in the woods and decides to take her into his abode. The humans soon find her with the wolf. Even after the princess tells them that the Night Wolf had been nice to her, the humans don't believe her and they arrest the wolf, burning him in front of their palace.

The Game of the Night is adapted from the story, except that in this game, the Night Wolf doesn't get arrested. Instead, he kills all the humans. The legend considered as the origin of the wolves' hatred for humans. Only wolves know about the story and what it symbolizes in the world of shifters.

The invitation means only one thing—whoever just texted me is a wolf!

I click on the notification and realize I'm being redirected to a website called Games n' Fun. There I find an inbox with the two messages already waiting for me. Thinking about the possibility of being wrong about the identity of the unknown texter, I type in a message and press enter.

Hi, I'd like to play.

A few seconds of nothing. Then, I see Grindelvi is typing.

We have an inner room but before you can start the game, you have to introduce yourself to others. Are you an Ancient S or an Ancient Otherling?

I know what those two words mean, and it only heightens my suspicion that Grindelvi is one of us. An Ancient S is a code for a Night Shifter while an Ancient Otherling means human.

This texter is trying to find out if I'm a wolf too. A human will have no idea what those two words mean.

However, I have a suspicion that I'll still go through another test to prove my identity. What if I'm human but luckily pick that I'm an Ancient S? It's too risky to bring in a random human into the inner room and reveal the world of shifters to them.

I'm an Ancient S.

Good. Click the link I'll drop in your inbox now.

Two seconds later, I'm staring at a link in my inbox. My heart slams against my ribcage as I click on it. What exactly will I find in there? A group of werewolves who might have information about Adeline's pack? Will I be kicked out as soon as I fail the second test, ending up with nothing but an inbox and a stranger's username, Grindelvi?

As soon as I enter the room, the inbox's background

changes to that of a snarling wolf. A message appears on my screen.

Welcome, Luke H. to the inner room, an online community of Ancient S. You must share your story with everyone before you play the Game of the Night.

CHAPTER 8

ADELINE

"Luke? Hello?"

I move to the door of the apartment again and rap on the wood, waiting for a few seconds before concluding he isn't home.

It's been six minutes since I arrived and the morning sun stinging the back of my neck deepens the burning sensation of embarrassment.

What did I expect? That a man like Luke would give me his home address and patiently wait for my visit?

Partly, this is my fault. I should have given Luke a call before hopping on a bus and coming to his small apartment in Falview Street. Now I'm embarrassed that I'd brought myself here to meet an empty apartment.

Luke lives in a residential building on the second floor. Each floor has separate long verandahs with metal railings that over-look the building's parking lot and standing beside a blue sedan is a middle-aged man who's been staring at me since I started knocking on Luke's door.

"Miss? Are you looking for someone?" he calls out.

I break into a smile and hope my stinging cheeks haven't turned red from shame. "Luke Holland? Is he home?"

The man scratches his eyebrow. "He's hardly home but I saw him come in last night. I'm his neighbor on the left."

"Oh." My eyes dart to the next apartment after Luke's. 9A. "Do you know when he's going to be back? Can you tell him Adeline stopped by?"

The man shakes his head and opens the door of his sedan. "I said he's hardly home. Not trying to ruin anything but that man scares the shit out of me. I'm even surprised he's got someone visiting him. Goodbye, miss."

He gets into his sedan, starts the car and backs out of the parking lot. The man's words leave me bewildered. Why doesn't Luke have anyone visiting him? And why is Luke's neighbor scared of him?

The very moment I met Luke, I could tell he was a man of secrets. His mystery intrigued me. It was the reason I found myself talking to him, trying to reach for those thick layers of his obscurity, tearing them down one after the other.

But Luke is an unending maze of secrets. I don't know who he really is and it scares me that the revelation I just got from his neighbor would change my perspective of him. Or not.

Should I really care about Luke's secrets? Every other thing about him is a breath of wonder. From his mesmerizing looks to his heated touch, Luke makes my desires flutter on clouds of unfiltered delight, capturing me in the warmth of what he possesses. He matches my definition of peace. Bliss. Everything that speaks of tranquility in the midst of a roaring storm.

His secrets don't matter. Not when the feelings are this strong.

I reach for my phone in my bag and call Luke. It goes to voicemail immediately. *Hello, I'm not available right now. Leave a message and I'll get back to you as soon as I get it.*

His deep voice whispers over my skin, as if he can touch me without even being close, sizzling the pit of my belly and reminding me exactly why I'm here. I miss him. How he makes me feel. How I love making him feel.

Disappointed, I slip my phone into my jacket pocket and leave Luke's empty apartment.

The next stop I make is to the bar. Several of my kind are inside, gathering at their usual tables and drinking like they can see extra lives at the bottom of their glasses. The usual noise. The loud jabs. I hate to be here right now but I trudge ahead, toward the counter, head bowed and my heart coated with loneliness.

I ignore two werewolves who shout lewd comments at me, too bothered by Luke's absence to care about them. I'm only here for a drink. Maybe I'll find comfort at the pit of my tumbler, too.

"They're new in town," my favorite cousin, Carl, says when I get to the counter. He's cleaning beer mugs and staring at the catcalling wolves in disgust.

"Ah, that's why they don't know Lawrence will claw their faces if they make a move on me."

"I don't like them," my cousin admits. His eyes return to his mugs but I can still sense his swirling desperation to kick these mannerless wolves out of his bar. "They're loud and don't know when to shut up. I can't wait for your brothers to come in and make them shit their pants."

His joke gets a shrug from me. I clasp my hands, place them on the counter and release a deep sigh. I'd imagined the visit to Luke's apartment would go a little differently. Having a talk while I got lost in his eyes, his delicious lips moving without me catching any single word. Then I would've taken a bold step of kissing him as I found that strong Adeline he brings out in me. He would've led me to the bed and we'd tangle in the sheets, my lips burning with every call of his name.

"Are you alright?" Carl's voice interrupts my thoughts of Luke fucking me in his apartment.

"I'm good," I quickly answer.

I'm not. I want Luke more than the oxygen I breathe. He's the one who leads me to unexplored realms. He's heaven on...

Stop it, Addy! Or you're going to lose yourself.

"The Addy I know never says I'm good," Carl says, arching an eyebrow. "She just folds her arms, raises an eyebrow and asks you why you think she isn't alright. Always a question to answer a question."

A scoff escapes my lips as I cross my arms. "Why do you think I'm not alright?"

Carl picks up another mug and begins to clean it. "Don't bullshit me. You're too late with the usual question. Are you alright?"

I drop my arms and know that it's time to tell my cousin the truth. When I let out another sigh, my bottom lip pushes out, diverting the airflow to my bangs. "I miss someone."

"Aha." Carl grins, his eyes narrowing as a gleam of curiosity settles in them. "You have a boy on your mind. Who is he?"

"He's a new guy in town. You met him a few days ago."

"I meet a lot of new guys and wolves." Carl eyes the loud wolves again. "Some of them I don't want to meet again."

I laugh, sensing my loaded heart take a dive to 'relief street'. Don't think about Luke's empty apartment for now. Think about why you like him.

"He's nothing like them."

"Interesting. What does he look like?"

"A work of fascinating art. I could spend hours just describing his eyes and what they do to me," I answer, elbow on the counter and hand resting on my cheek.

Carl's eyes widen. "Oh, that smile! You like this wolf. Why do I not remember him?"

I roll my eyes and take my hand from my cheek, poking the counter's hard surface with my index finger. "Anniversary? You thought he was married but it was the anniversary of his father's death? Ring a bell?"

Carl snaps his finger. "I remember him now! Oh, Addy, I thought it was going to be a one night thing."

I nod repeatedly. "I thought the same but here I am still thinking of him. Carl, he's so amazing. I've never met a man like him."

Carl lowers his eyebrows as he leans forward, dropping the napkin in his hand on the counter. He's concerned about something. I know what's coming.

The men in my family have never disappointed me when it comes to displaying their blind care for me. Carl is no exception. He may prefer spending his days pouring drinks for wolves and unsuspecting humans but he's also like my overprotective brothers.

The only difference is he's a little less annoying than Lawrence and Damian and he knows when to give up trying to be protective.

"Do you know anything about him?"

I twist my lips to the left, my eyes darting up as I garner the little information I have on Luke in my head. This shouldn't be hard. I even know where he lives!

"I do." Then I proceed to tell Carl about Luke's grandmother and his apartment. No mention of Luke's neighbor. Not even that I have suspicions he's hiding something from me.

Why can't you tell me everything that's eating you from the inside, Luke? I can see the pain in your eyes. I can see the ocean of your ache threatening to drown you.

"Have you told your brothers about him?"

"Carl, you know they're the last people who should ever find out about this."

Carl smiles and picks up his napkin. "Your secret's safe with me."

"What? You're not going to tell me to stop seeing him?"

Carl flings the napkin over his shoulder. "If he makes you smile, why would I want to wipe it off your face?"

His words almost bring tears to my eyes. The very words I want to hear.

"But be careful. New wolves are always up to no good when they come here. They have a chip on their shoulder because they're running from their shitty lives in their former towns. Maybe this Luke is different but whoever he is, Addy, don't think he's completely flawless."

I mull over the words and as I walk out of Moonlit a few hours later, knowing what I need to do next.

Find out who the hell Luke Holland is.

The second test is harder.

I draw the scent of pine into my lungs as I glance around, waiting to find out exactly what the second test is. As I stand in the heart of the woods, warm sunshine prickles my exposed skin, reminding me that I have no clothes on.

Grindelvi didn't ask me to meet him at a park or something. In fact, I was instructed to take a bus from Falview to a different street called Gaski, then from Gaski back to Falview, stop at the community's library and trek to the edge of town.

From there, I'd find the woods. *Go into the woods. Switch off your phone and strip down to nothing. Wait for someone to get you.*

Which brought me to this moment. Alone in a forest, alert. Naked.

Being naked isn't embarrassing. It's the thought of finding out this is some prank being pulled by a group of humans that is.

As a shifter, each time you morph into your wolf form you reveal your nudity to the dark, the dusk, or whatever time it is.

It's our way of life and having to wait butt naked in the middle of nowhere isn't at all shameful.

Come to think of it, I've never explored these woods. Since I came to Falview, I've rarely had time to shift at night and run in the woods, howling until I reach peak power. Blood rushing. Energy vibrating. The core of my being complete.

I miss running. Just standing in the midst of a land typical of my kind, I want to dash into the woods, feeling my muscles tightening, bones reforming, claws shooting out of my fingers, fur covering me like a blanket and teeth taking shape into fangs.

My ears pick up footsteps to my left. I glance in that direction, fingers spread out to attack. I'll only reveal my fangs when I'm sure the person approaching is a shifter.

A familiar scent hits my nostrils. It's the one every wolf wears. Blood that stinks of brotherliness. A connection so strong I retract my fingers and let my hands drop to my side. Just then, a man steps out from the woods.

I size him up in one cursory look. The newcomer looks like he's seen better days, his thin frame the resemblance of a man with an eating disorder. His collarbones stick out above the neckline of his blue shirt while his slim fitted jeans cling to the length of his spindly legs. His green eyes study me, nose flaring at the same time to catch my scent.

"Get dressed and come with me."

I pick up my clothes, cautiously keeping an eye on him. Who is he? Where's he leading me? He turns in the direction he came as soon as I don the last of my clothes. I quickly follow him into the woods. He's not someone I know but the known smell of a shifter surrounds him.

Werewolves, especially ones who want to keep their identity hidden, mask their smell by wearing enchanted perfumes. These perfumes are created by the North End witches, a generation of human sorcerers who have been working with the were-wolves for centuries.

I used an enchanted perfume and the wolf walking in front of me must have prepared himself for it. That's why I had been ordered to go naked. Being naked makes for a faster whiff of my wolf smell.

Without a perfume, Adeline and my brothers would have caught my scent. My plan would have ended before it even started. Adeline, on the other hand, doesn't use one. She isn't hiding from anyone. Other shifters know who she is. Her family controls most of the packs in the area. What's the need for an enchanted perfume?

The lanky wolf turns a corner and heads for a river. As I follow him, I tune out the noise of the woods and try to focus on him. Steady heartbeat. Measured footsteps. Brown hair that smells of the open air as though he's been living in the woods all his life. I let my eyes trail his body, the pores of his skin, the muscles throbbing in...

"I'm Grindelvi," the lanky man interrupts, suddenly stopping and turning to face me.

I almost crash into him. "Sorry! Oh, hey, Grindelvi."

"You're reading me," he observes, his green eyes sharp.

Yes, I'm reading him, literally. That way, I can tell which pack he's from and possibly connect with his mind to know his real name.

Only a few wolves have mastered the art of reading another. I'm one of the special ones. My father taught me how to read other wolves without their knowledge. But if the wolf being studied is a special wolf too, they can tell when they are being read.

Grindelvi knew I was reading him. He's no ordinary wolf. He's like me.

"Yes," I admit. "Someone must have taught you too."

A corner of Grindelvi's mouth stretches to a grin. He turns around and starts walking again. "Yeah, some of us have been attentive in class."

"Not all wolves can learn it."

"I know that Luke H.," Grindelvi replies. "That's why you and I are very special."

"Call me Luke. My name is Luke."

"Okay, Luke," Grindelvi says.

"Why do I have to meet with the group?" I ask him, trying to keep pace with him. "I already told you my story. Is there something I'm here to do?"

Grindelvi doesn't speak for a few seconds. He tucks a strand of his long brown hair behind his ear and answers, "Yeah, touching story but we need to know you. If you want to play the Game of the Night, you have to meet the other players."

This is more than playing an online game, I'm sure of it. Yesterday, I spent two hours chatting with the other players in the inner room, telling them the story about my pack, avoiding the details like my father's name and where my pack had been located.

Some group members said it's a sad story. They all admitted their hatred for the High Ridge Pack. I'd connected with that hatred. We had common ground. I'd started to think that I was in.

Then I woke up this morning to Grindelvi's message to meet the group followed by my ass baking in the sun. These people want to keep their location hidden, especially from the High Ridge Pack. Any sane group that hates them will do the same.

"Here we are," Grindelvi says, stepping into a clearing.

Sitting in the center is a campsite with a few werewolves and a single tent. Two women with matching pink hair, studded noses and lips, biker pants and jackets, sit on a tree trunk, watching me as I continue to follow Grindelvi into the place. Twins?

At the entrance of the tent is a buff male wolf, arms crossed and his milky eyes staring into nothing and I realize he's blind. It's impossible to imagine what I would be without my eyesight. Lost in eternal darkness. Unable to gaze upon Adeline's alluring face, only sensing her magnetic presence. At the same time, my blindness would have saved me from seeing the horrific slaughtering of my pack.

"This is Jack," Grindelvi says to me as we approach the blind wolf. "He's the camp's watch guard. Ironic, isn't it? He can't see shit."

"Yeah, how does he protect you?"

Jack is the one who answers me. "My other senses work better than that of a seeing wolf."

"Nice meeting you, Jack," I extend a hand for a shake but the muscular wolf doesn't take it.

"Those are Fena and Brena," Grindelvi says, pointing to the pink-haired female wolves. "And no, they're not twins."

Fena and Brena wave to me at the same time. Then they drop their hands, eyes still carefully watching me.

"Is this the whole camp?" I inquire.

It is disappointing enough that I'd stayed in the woods naked to meet four wolves. I'd been expecting a full pack. Maybe warrior wolves. People who are ready to beat the daylight out of the High Ridge wolves.

"No." Grindelvi leads me into the tent.

That's it? No further response? Maybe the tent is a magical portal into the actual camp full of wolves.

But I'm met with another disappointment. The tent is empty, save for four beds, a wooden chair, hunting weapons and some clothes.

"We're at the mouth of the camp," Grindelvi says, settling in the wooden chair. "You have to accept our rules and reveal your true identity before you meet the rest of the group."

"I told you everything about me. What else do you want to know?"

Grindelvi smiles. "Why don't we start from the beginning, Luke?"

They embrace me. Every one of them.

For the first time in five years, I'm part of a family—the Blood Born Pack.

It almost brings me to tears. The love. The smiles. The strong connection building inside me.

"Welcome, Luke," the pack leader, Arthur, says to me.

He's the last to hug me. A gray-haired six-foot wolf who watched his own pack suffer and die at the hands of the High Ridge wolves. As the Alpha, he'd been away on a mission to seek new grounds for his pack when they were attacked.

"The High Ridge Pack have been invading other packs for years. They don't care about anyone. They don't respect pack ties. They're only greedy for our lands. We've been able to gather as many affected wolves as we could. This is everyone for now."

I see men and women who have lost their homes, cubs separated from their parents, warriors who are battling the guilt of not being able to fight back. The sight is heartbreaking. It squeezes my heart until I have no strength to hide my pain. Like being pushed against a wall by a reality that doesn't want to let me go.

As soon as the pack leader gathers the camp for dinner, I dash out of the area and into the woods, running until I lose track of time.

The pain trails me. It's the silent footsteps in the woods, drowned out by the sound of my own. I can sense it gaining on me. Reaching for my sanity. Awakening my bottled-up emotions.

When pain does catch up, I fall to my knees, releasing an agonizing howl that reverberates through the woods. Every hurtful memory unites in one heart-wrenching inferno, consuming me until it steals the howl from my throat. I fold at the waist and drop my hands to the ground. My body rakes with spasms as I try to catch my breath.

"Have you let it all out?"

I spin around to see one of the pink-haired female wolves standing behind me. I don't know who it is. Fena? Brena?

She walks toward me, a half-smile playing across her lips. The studs on her nose and lips glint under the light of the half-moon. Wait, it's already dark? How long have I been running?

"We all feel what you feel," the female wolf says.

I'm not sure they do. My tears can't erase the pain. My howls can't contain the ache. I'm the only one living this and the Blood Born Pack are just wolves who share the same sad story.

"Which one are you?"

"Fena."

"Let me guess, Arthur asked you to follow me?"

Fena shrugs and folds her arms. "Kinda. We don't want wolves leaving the camp without telling someone."

I scoff and get to my feet. "I'm not going to tell anyone about the camp. The High Ridge Pack took my family too."

Fena shakes her head. "It's not that. You don't understand how dangerous these people are. They search the woods every night for wolves. They just haven't found out where we are."

"That's... Wolves have a way of discovering packs. It's

strange, or damn fucking lucky, that the camp hasn't been discovered."

Fena's half smile returns. "No, we're under ancient protection. Arthur isn't the only pack leader. A more powerful wolf is protecting us."

I raise an eyebrow at her. "What wolf?"

Fena's answer is interrupted by a barrage of howls. The wailing wolves sound very close and the fear that creeps into Fena's eyes tells me they're not from her pack.

"Quick! Let's get back!"

We race to the camp together, Fena glancing over her shoulder the whole way as if she's expecting to be attacked. There, Fena tells Arthur the High Ridge wolves are in the woods again.

"No one leaves the camp until morning," Arthur announces to everyone.

His hazel eyes settle on me. Arthur possesses such an authoritative aura around him that it's hard to picture a more powerful wolf ordering him around. Who is the actual leader of the Blood Born Pack?

"Your best shot at staying alive is here. If you go out to the woods alone, you'll find nothing but a bunch of mindless wolves who will end your life," the pack leader states flatly.

Staying alive is my priority. Ending up dead means my pack's death will go in vain. *Yeah, Arthur, I understand.*

I go to sit with some wolves around a campfire and one of them offers me a beer. I thank him after taking the drink. The men talk about the wolves from the High Ridge Pack and how they'll enjoy ripping their bodies apart when they win the pack wars.

My mind immediately goes to Adeline. She's from the same pack everyone is out to get. I can't bear the thought of someone tearing her into pieces, her perfect wolf form becoming nothing but a litter of bones, flesh and blood.

I have to take her away from her people. Sounds ridiculous but it's the only way. Adeline doesn't deserve to die for the sins of her pack.

I pull out my phone from my pocket to text Adeline. *Wanna see a movie with me? Is tomorrow night okay?*

Her response is immediate, as if she's been waiting to get a text from me. *Sure! Tomorrow night is okay.*

"Your girl?" The wolf who had handed me the beer asks, a mischievous grin spreading across his face.

"Uh?" I say, slipping my phone back into my pocket.

"You're smiling."

He's right. It's already stretching to the ends of my mouth, the thought of seeing Adeline tomorrow night bursting in my heart.

"Yeah," I say, bringing the bottle to my lips. "She's my girl."

CHAPTER 10
ADELINE

Luke is standing outside my house. A gun is in his face.
"Move the fuck back," Damian's tone is as harsh as
the biting look in his eyes, like staring into the depth
of a freezing whirlpool.

I've never seen him this angry. Damian isn't...totally sane.
He does very irrational things that makes me scared of him all
the more.

My family knows he's unstable but we pretend and over-
look his batty acts. Even when we try to help him, Damian
reminds us that he doesn't have a screw loose. Then he goes out
to do something totally out of this world.

His behavior rarely surprises us and I have never been this
scared of what he could do up until this point. But the gun
doesn't waver from Luke's face.

Damian turns his face to the left to spit into the trimmed
grass of the mansion's lawn. "You heard me? Back off," Damian
repeats.

"Easy, man," Luke says, his hands in the air. "I'm only here
for Adeline."

"Damian, lower the gun, please!" I beg, daring to grab my brother by the arm.

He glances at me, face creased into a deep frown that shows he's about to lose his shit. "This isn't your business, Addy."

It is my business! Luke's here because I'd invited him. I was thrilled to see his message yesterday, asking me to see a movie. He's finally taking me on a date! I didn't think twice before replying that I would love to. Then he asked for my house address and I gave it to him.

The first problem is Luke's decision to drive to my family's mansion, knock on the front door and ask to see me. He did get a response but it was from my brother, a mad man holding a gun to his face.

"Seriously, just drop the gun," I tell Damian again.

He isn't listening. Damian takes a step forward and presses the muzzle of the shotgun to Luke's chest. A gasp escapes my lips.

Luke does nothing but lower his gaze to the gun. He looks up at Damian, the corners of his lips arching to form a slow grin. The cold response has my pulse stuttering. Luke almost looks as if he wants this...

"Damian!" A voice booms from inside the house.

My oldest brother, Lawrence, steps out of the house. His displeasure burns in his eyes as he moves swiftly to Damian, bending the barrel of the shotgun to the back. The action angers Damian and he tosses the damaged gun aside, shaking his fist at Lawrence.

"That's my gun!"

"Well, it's gone now. Deal with it," Lawrence sneers at him. "Go inside and don't come out!"

Damian grumbles something and throws one final glare at Luke. He turns around and storms inside, slamming the door so hard the thick glass panels at its center rattle.

Lawrence faces Luke and me. His smile is puzzlingly warm. "Sorry about that."

Lawrence is as insane as Damian but somehow, my oldest brother can put a leash on his madness. At the same time, he's the only one who knows how to control Damian, like a puppet while he holds the strings.

"Have we met?" Lawrence adds.

The question heightens my fear. Suddenly, I wish Damian was still pointing the gun at Luke and Lawrence was inside the house, staying out of this. If he remembers I met Luke at the bar the other night, he won't let him out of here, not alive!

"I don't think so," Luke answers as if he can hear my silent prayers that Lawrence doesn't remember him. "Or your brother wouldn't be pointing a gun at me."

Lawrence scoffs. He puts his hands in his pockets and grins at Luke. "Are you scared of a gun?"

A stupid question! Luke's human. He isn't anything like me. One shot and I'll be weeping over his dead body.

"It's a gun," Luke replies. "Who isn't scared of a gun?"

Lawrence folds his arms. "Hm, because I could swear for a second there that you didn't move an inch when Damian pointed the shotgun at you."

I quickly step between them. "Lawrence, please, I really need to get going. Luke is taking me out to see a movie."

Lawrence doesn't object. I expect him to flare up and tell me to get back into the house. He just smiles again and says to Luke, "Take care of my sister. If anything happens to her," he pokes the air in Luke's direction, "I'm coming for you."

My belly bubbles for joy, sending a smile to my face, one I can't contain. He just gave me the green light to go out with Luke! I grab Luke by the arm and pull him out of there before Lawrence can change his mind.

"Is this your car?" I ask Luke as soon as we get to a red Ford parked outside my family mansion.

"It's Jacqueline's." Luke holds the door for me. "Come on."

Luke starts the car and drives away. Lawrence is still standing in front of the house, hands in the pockets of his pants, eyes trailing the car as we leave.

I don't know what to think of his strange attitude. He allowed me to leave with Luke and even destroyed Damian's shotgun to defend him. Is Lawrence losing his cruelty or is this another mind game to bend me to his will?

"Your brothers are creepy," Luke finally says as we hit the main road to the cinema. "Are they always protective of you?"

I nod. "They've always been like that, but it got worse after my mom died."

"Oh." Luke doesn't look at me. "I'm sorry to hear about that."

"It's okay. I try not to think about her death."

It happened five years ago. I was sobbing in my room because Lawrence wouldn't let me out of the house again.

At about eight in the evening, the piercing howl of my father filled the whole mansion, rattling the windows, enveloping the pack area in one mournful tone and causing the other wolves to respond in a loud chorus of howls. I instantly knew something was wrong.

I raced out of my room, screeched to a stop at the foot of the grand stairway as though I'd slammed my face into an invisible wall. The bloody body of my mother in the arms of my weeping father.

To this day, I have no idea who or what killed her. My father, Jordan, the Alpha of High Ridge Pack, refuses to share the details of her death with me. Not a single detail.

"It's sad, Addy," he'll always say. "I don't want to talk about it."

He didn't even tell his sons. I'm not sure about Lawrence though, because I caught him one night with one of his friends talking about the High Wolf and how he had attacked my father.

"Who's the High Wolf?" I'd asked before Lawrence slammed the door in my face.

It's been five years and I'm still mourning the death of a woman who deeply loved me. She was the only one who could reign Lawrence and Damian in. What's more, when Mom was alive, I was a free bird, spreading my wings with no fear of falling. After her death, I found myself in the cage my brothers had put me in. No mother. No one to love me like she did.

No one to love back.

"It hurts when you lose the people you love," Luke says in a low voice.

His eyes are fixed on the road. Since I told him about my mother, he's barely looked at me. Does he feel sorry for me? If he is, I don't want his pity. I'm fine.

"It really hurts but we have to get over it," I tell him. "I'm trying to move on—it's what she'd want."

"It's not that easy!" Luke snaps.

His hands tighten around the steering wheel, his knuckles turning red. His chin trembles, followed by the grumble that reverberates through his chest.

"What's wrong?" I ask, not understanding what's just happened.

"Nothing."

I keep quiet and turn my face away, looking out the window. The crisp night air caresses my face, battling the sensation of unhappiness that fills me. Except it does nothing to take the feeling away.

Luke is right next to me but I sense his mind is a million

miles away, embracing the misery he doesn't want to talk about.

I was looking forward to tonight. My stomach tingled every time I thought about it, the sensation spreading lower and lower. I remembered the attraction. The chemistry. The way he makes me feel. But now, it's clear I don't know how to get him talking. His firm response bears a deeper message—back off.

A stray tear spills down my cheek. I sweep it away with my thumb before it can drip into the fabric of my satin blouse.

I'll take my time. Luke will eventually open up, I'm sure of it. Not even the strongest person in the world can hold their pain without falling under the weight of its chaotic emotions.

O f all the movies to see, it had to be *Titanic*.
It is one of the world's most tear-jerking love stories ever captured. The whole thing is tragic. If only Rose knew she would live to spend the rest of her life without Jack, she wouldn't have given the good-looking man a chance to steal her heart.

It's awkward as I sit in the movie theater, watching Jack and Rose's on-screen affair while my off-screen affair is nothing but a shot in the dark.

I've started something I don't know the end of. Are my feelings for Luke leading me anywhere? He's a walking mystery. An impregnable wall of secrets. If at this point he's unwilling to tell me anything, then there's no chance for our romance.

Maybe unlike Rose, I should let go of my feelings and let them sink to the bottom of the ocean. I'll be saving myself from the clutches of harsh loneliness. I'll be surviving the unceasing thoughts in my head trying to understand Luke's silence and I'll find love again.

I steal a glance at him. His eyes are glued to the screen, his lips pursed as if the love tale infuriates him. He doesn't know that his silence is killing me.

Did I say anything wrong in the car? Is this about Damian pointing a gun at him?

"Luke," I whisper his name but he doesn't hear me. Or he's pretending not to.

I touch his arm. He looks at me. There's something strange in his gaze. Like I'm seeing his pain for the first time.

"I'm sorry about everything, Luke. I told you my family is overprotective but I didn't know Damian would threaten you with a gun. If you don't want to see me anymore, I'll understand your decision. I mean, I wouldn't want to stay with a woman with crazy brothers either."

His green eyes appear to glint for a second. Then he flicks a tear from my cheek, one that I hadn't been aware of shedding. He leans forward, his eyes softening in a way that takes my breath away. "It's okay, Addy. I'm not angry."

With a ghost of a smile, Luke turns his head to focus on the screen again. My hand remains on his arm and he doesn't make any attempt to pull away.

Somehow, his answer melts the heaviness in my heart like an iceberg being kissed by the warm rays of the sun. The glint I'd briefly seen in Luke's eyes lights my dark mind. Gradually. Completely.

Without warning, I place my head on his shoulder and intertwine my arm with his, digging my fingers into the fold of his biceps. He freezes but before I can wonder why, his chin moves over my head, possibly bringing himself to look at me. The movement is followed by the brush of his lips against my forehead.

He just kissed me!

I close my eyes to contain the explosion of delight. My heart thumps in my chest. A warm sensation ripples through my body straight to the tips of my fingers.

Only Luke has the power to make me feel this way.

I might be naive like my family says, and yes, Luke has secrets, but this thing we have, it's bigger than any of that. It has to be.

I stroke his arm gently, rubbing my cheek against his shoulder like a doting cat. Except that touch isn't enough. I want to show him what he does to me. That I can't keep my hand off him. My other hand reaches for his shirt, fingers calmly unbuttoning it, and he doesn't stop me. One. Two. Three buttons undone.

I touch the deeply cut and well-grooved chest, thumb trailing the magnificence he possesses. When my fingers brush against his nipple slightly, Luke's body responds with a jerk. A low groan soon slips out of him, immediately warming the insides of my thighs.

My eyes are still closed when I feel his hand on my lap. It doubles the fiery explosion between my legs, as if I'd just been set ablaze. But by a delightful fire. A fire that loves me.

In the dimness of the theater, Luke's fingers crawl under my skirt, tugging at the side of my panties. My breath shudders with every move he makes. I try to hold my gasps but it's impossible not to let them out as Luke continues to probe underneath.

His fingers soon find my pussy, separating the folds to find the quivering flesh inside. He strokes me gently while my hand finds his lap, his erection obvious in his jeans. His breath is hot against my neck as he deepens his fingers. My body trembles uncontrollably, accepting the ocean of joy washing over me.

Luke groans and whispers quietly, "Fuck, I can't stop touching you."

Elation threatens to tear my abdomen apart as he echoes

the same thoughts I had only moments ago. Shivers of ecstasy hit me like small earthquakes. In the depths of my belly, a burning pleasure is born, aiming for my heart and fighting to burst out.

The story of Jack and Rose plays before me, but I see them no more. Instead, my happiness plays in front of me. Every touch is searing my mind, every movement one I'll never forget.

Luke's fingers explore my clit. Fondling it. Molding me.

I grab his arm like a lifeline and try to close my legs to control the flow of heat spreading across my body. From the crown of my head to the tip of my toes.

"Easy," he whispers in a deep voice.

Thankfully, we're the only ones on our row or the way I constantly shift in my seat would give me away.

"God," I blurt out but it isn't loud.

With ever increasing speed Luke strokes me. His own breathing increases and it spurs me on, now lost in the sensations as his expert fingers drive me to heaven and back. The breathless pleasure clamps around my groin, then my stomach, then ripples up my whole torso. I arch my back as it releases, exploding like a supernova.

One that has to fall apart in complete silence.

I return to Earth slowly, my body trembling from the experience. Drawing in a shuddering breath, I wrap my arms around Luke, blinking at the screen.

Luke pleasured me in a room full of people. No one saw anything. Barely a sound was made. The thought of it makes me giggle.

I've never done this. Everything about Luke rings of exploration and that's because he keeps taking me to realms I've never been before. Trying out new things with me.

I think it's high time I admitted the truth.

I'm falling for Luke Holland.

The end credits of Titanic are still rolling by the time we walk out of the movie theater.

My body pulsates with excitement, thinking about what Luke had done to me in the dim theater. Swirls of sensation embrace my belly every single time I remember his fingers exploring me, drawing silent moans out of me.

I hold his hand as we move toward his car, wondering if I should tell him that I loved what we did. I want us to do it again. Maybe in the car. Maybe in the warmth of his bedroom.

When I glance at him, Luke's staring straight ahead. He hasn't spoken a word since he made me come in the theater. It's as if he doesn't want to talk about it.

Immediately, my excitement vanishes like smoke lost in the wind. Luke probably pleasured me because he felt I wanted it. Not because he wanted it, too.

The thought stings my eyes. I'm embarrassed. Angry. Confused. I'm everything at once.

I take my hand away from his and tuck my hands under my arms. An invisible cold attacks me—rather, Luke's silence instills the cold in me. Deeply. Painfully.

"What's wrong?" he says, his voice harsh when he stops to address me.

I peer into his eyes, seeing them burn with rage. What's his problem? Why is he so angry? "Did that mean nothing to you?"

He freezes. "It doesn't matter what it means to me."

I draw back sharply. "Of course it does. I haven't done anything like that with anyone, Luke. Ever."

"Enough with the lies, Adeline!" He presses the heels of his palms into his temples. "You just let me get you off in a movie theater. You're far from some naive virgin."

Heat stings my cheeks as shame burns me from the inside out. "I was a virgin," I whisper. "You were my first, Luke."

It's his turn to look as if he's just been slapped. Possessiveness flares in his green gaze. A burst of lust. But then he's shaking his head. "Did your brothers tell you to say that?"

"What the hell do they have to do with this?"

Luke closes his eyes. I see his chin tremble, his jawline jutting out in annoyance. When he opens his eyes again, the fire in them is ten times fiercer. "Don't act like you don't know what your brothers are."

His reply takes me off guard. "What are you talking about?"

"I know what you are!" Luke snaps.

He moves closer to me, the gorgeous face I've come to love now transforming into one that scares me. I've never seen him this angry.

"I know what you all are," he growls.

My lips quiver as I struggle to respond. Is Luke talking about my true identity? If so, how in the world did he find out?

"How..." I stutter. "How do you know we're shifters?"

His next reaction sends my heart straight to my mouth. Luke pins me to the side of the car, his face so close to mine, I get a plain view of the fury dancing in his eyes. His hand closes around my neck but his grip isn't tight, as though he's careful not to hurt me.

"I know more than that, Adeline. I'm a shifter, too. Don't act so innocent. I watched your pack kill my family."

His revelation deals the final blow. I can't take in what he just said. He's a shifter? My family killed his pack?

I'm too stunned to speak. It's like my lips are sealed by the heavy grip of shock, burying my words of denial.

This can't be real! It's not real! Luke's been lying to me. He knew what I was and said nothing. He kept his pain from me when, in my own ignorance, my family was responsible for it.

He takes his hand away from my neck and steps back. The fury in his eyes disappears as though someone has raised the curtain from his clouded mind, showing him what he's doing.

As I watch him, tears roll down my cheeks uncontrollably. My heart is heavier than a rock. Pain crawls up my body as though someone has set me ablaze. I shake my head, trying to kick his confession out of my head. He's lying. Luke is messing with me.

"You didn't know, did you?" Luke asks.

But I'm not listening to him anymore. I just want to get out of here. Away from him.

When I go to move, Luke grabs my arms and makes me face him again. "You didn't know, did you?"

I soon find my voice. "You're lying. My family would never do that to you."

"They did. They killed my family. I watched them do it."

I break free from his grip, wiping my face with the back of my hand. "You're lying. Who are you? What's the name of your pack? Where are you from?"

Luke sighs, pressing his fingers into his temples. "Is that necessary?"

"I demand to know!" I yell.

The tables have turned. I'm the one boiling with rage now.

"Okay," Luke answers. "I'm Luke Holland, the only surviving member of the Black Diamond pack. Five years ago, the High Ridge pack stormed into my pack and killed every wolf, including my father and the mate I was supposed to marry."

CHAPTER 11
LUKE

Her clothes are the first to come off.

They fall to the wet ground, circling her feet just as the first strands of fur begin to shoot out of her skin. The hair spreads up her body, her curvy form, her gorgeous face until a different being is staring back at me, eyes inky with pain.

The Adeline before me is the real one, naked in the actual form she was born. No long hair. No deceitful human skin. Just her. The werewolf.

"Adeline," I call her name just as she dashes into the night on all fours.

The theater is beside a forest and so it awards her a chance to shift in a flash and run into the trees. I glance around, noting we're alone.

And that I have a choice.

With a groan I shift too, shedding my clothes the same way Addy did. My muscled frame changes into a bigger one, fur replacing my skin, eyes adjusting to the cloak of the night.

I can see everything now, sense all, hear all; the clicking of a woman's stilettos on the tarred road, the gray-haired man smoking in his car at the mall a block away, people's emotions as loud as the throbbing of a heart and the stench of their bodies clouding my nostrils.

But they don't matter. I want to think about Adeline. Only her.

In my wolf form, I try to find Addy in the chaos of emotions hitting me. Weaving through the feelings. Moving past the reactions.

Then I find her. She's a bundle of pain, an overwhelmed mass of hurt. Adeline's agony is raw. Uncontrollable.

I connect with her mind. She's racing in the bushes close to the movie theater, heart thumping.

I follow suit, jumping into the thick cluster of wild plants and catching up with her. Adeline growls at me as soon as she sees me, a clear sign that I should go away.

Which I'm not going to do.

In our wolf forms, we can't communicate like humans. Instead, we speak with our minds. A telepathic channel that strengthens our ties as kindred beings.

"Adeline!"

"Go away!"

She stops at the foot of a tree but won't look at me. Her rage burns me. I can sense every inch of it.

"You need to listen to me. You can't tell your brothers about me."

"Don't I deserve to know the truth?"

"Yes, you deserve the truth but if your brothers find out about me, I'm dead. The others are going to die, too."

That's when she turns to look at me.

"What others?"

"There's a new pack I joined. They're called the Blood Born pack. These wolves are born from pain, the pain that your family caused them. My pack wasn't the only one destroyed by yours. There are

several others and the Blood Born are a group of survivors who watched their loved ones die."

My answer only worsens her agony. I can feel Adeline struggling to silence the howl that threatens to come out of her.

"It can't be."

"It's the truth. I can take you to the pack right now and you can see for yourself. But I need you not to tell your brothers anything. They must not find out about me and the Blood Born Pack."

"Fine. I won't tell them about you. But I need to figure this out on my own. I don't even know you. Please, don't come looking for me."

My heart shatters as I watch her run away and out of sight. Shards of pain sting my heart until I feel the overwhelming need to yowl.

I push away the primal urge. Not now. I turn around and go back to my car, shifting as soon as I see the Ford.

My clothes are still where I left them. Adeline's too. After getting dressed, I pick them up, throw them into the backseat and back out of the movie theater parking lot.

I drive back to my apartment. Alone. Angry with myself. What have I done? Why couldn't I control my outbursts, the overpowering rage that made me yell at Adeline? I'm still thinking about her when I walk into my bedroom and flop down on my bed.

She didn't deserve what I did. And the truth is undeniable—she doesn't know what her family's been doing. It only deepens my guilt.

I'd touched her passionately in the movie theater, then torn by my complete lack of self-control around her, I pinned her to my car in the parking lot and made her feel bad for what her family had done to mine.

When I fondled Adeline, my fingers touching the wetness of her pussy, she had no idea what her reaction did to me. The way her eyes rolled back in her head, her thighs screaming to come together, her body shivering with mindless pleasure.

In no time, the blood rushed to my abdomen, tightening my cock until it was painful. I bit down on my groans, my insides a hot mess. Right there, I couldn't wait for the movie to end, so I could drive Adeline to my apartment and fuck her until it was impossible for her to be quiet.

My head drops into my hands, the second bombshell of truth ricocheting through me. Addy was a virgin. She gave herself to me because of the precious connection we've found, despite our circumstances.

Mine, my wolf growls. It wants to howl it into the night.

Except I've ruined everything. Adeline is never coming back to me. I'm sure of it. She won't want to believe her family is that cruel. Heck! I'd feel the same way too.

A light tap on my window catches my attention. I sit up in bed and stare at it, my nose immediately seeking any familiar smell of wolf.

It's definitely a wolf outside!

I rise to my feet, drawing out my claws and waiting for the slightest sign of an attack.

Tap. The sound again.

It takes me a few seconds to figure out someone is throwing something at my window. The next *tap* comes and I see a pebble fall on my windowsill.

Confused, I walk to my window and look outside. Standing in front of Jacqueline's Ford is Adeline, wearing a superman sweatshirt, her hands in the pockets of her baggy trousers.

Seeing her there, my heart takes a leap. It's like stepping away from the scorching sun and getting cool water sprayed on your stinging skin.

Then again, my pulse bursts into a gallop, palms turning moist as I pull open the window. I don't know what to expect from her. A mixture of bliss and uncertainty throb in my veins. Tingle the pit of my belly.

"Adeline?" My voice is barely a whisper.

She smiles. It touches my heart like a blast of warm light, melting my uncertainty.

"Can I come in?"

"Sure!" I quickly respond, bolting to my front door and opening it.

Her presence banishes the lonesome atmosphere in my apartment. I see it dissipating like a dark storm before the clear skies. It's the power of Adeline, her ability to bless me with her wonder without trying to.

"You came back?" I ask, closing the door quietly behind me.

Adeline faces me. I see a tear drop, making a dot on her gray sweatshirt. It breaks my heart to see her cry again.

When I reach forward to hold her, Adeline raises a hand and says, "I don't know what to think. It's hard to believe you. But at the same time I can't go home. I got these clothes from a kind woman who saw me weeping in front of her store. I don't have the strength to face my brothers."

"I understand, Adeline, and I don't blame you for not believing me. I should never have told you the way I did. I thought you knew."

Adeline breaks down into tears. Her body trembles with no control. Guilt squeezes my lungs as I try to speak, a lump of regret settling in my heart.

This is my fault.

I cross the room to her, reaching to hold her in my arms. Adeline moves closer, her body quivering with every ragged breath she takes.

"I'm sorry," the words come out of me, coated with the genuine guilt I feel.

"Can you just hold me?" Adeline whispers, pressing her teary face to my chest.

Her tears stain my shirt, salty water soaking into its fabric. They're the physical manifestation of her pain—my pain. As she sheds them, I sense tears gathering in my eyes too, ready to spill for as long as the truth makes me guilty.

"I'm so sorry," I repeat. "I thought you knew. I never planned to tell you this way."

Adeline doesn't say anything. Her sobs subside, coming in almost inaudible utters. She raises her head to look at me and up close, I see the pain filling her eyes.

"I'm sorry too, if that's what my family did," Adeline answers.

"You don't have to say sorry." I bring my face to her stained cheeks, kissing her tears softly. "You weren't a part of it."

"But they're my family."

"It's their sin, not yours."

Adeline is still looking at me. Her pain pulls me in, urging me to banish it. I lean in to brush my lips against hers, tasting her salty tears on them, her hot breath caressing my skin.

Raising her chin gently, I kiss her again, the action warming my insides and spreading through my body like waves. I hold my breath as I savor her mouth, touching the crook of her neck and sliding my other hand down the small of her back.

Adeline's small frame presses into mine. I can feel her soft breasts pressing against my chest, her nipples like tiny pebbles hiding beneath her sweatshirt. Moved by the growing passion, I slip a hand underneath her sweatshirt and find her right breast, fondling it gently.

A moan escapes her lips but I catch it with the kiss, swallowing her response. My other arm encircles her, holding her to my body as she starts shuddering. I thumb her nipple, stroking it, flicking it.

Adeline takes her mouth away from mine to whisper one word. "Yes."

Her voice deepens my desire, kindling my thirst like fire doused with fuel. I haul her against me, our panting bodies flush against each other.

Last time I was too blind to know the precious gift I was holding.

I won't make that mistake again.

CHAPTER 12

ADELINE

L uke lifts me up, letting me wrap my legs around his body. I throw my head back while he plants kisses on my body through the sweatshirt, walking towards his room. He kicks the door open, approaches his bed and gently sets me down.

Stepping away from me, he undresses, his eyes never leaving me. I worship every inch of skin as it's revealed, nothing but his naked body spiking my arousal. I don't know if he can spot the hunger in my own eyes, but the desperation to have him fucking me is raw, like I'm a tigress waiting to devour my prey.

He moves towards me and brings my hands to his butt cheeks, his throbbing cock facing me. My fingers dig into his ass, squeezing gently. Then I place a kiss on his abdomen, just above the scanty clump of hair on his pubic region. My mouth waters at the thought of tasting him.

"No, not tonight," he says, his voice gravelly. "Tonight is about me worshiping you."

Luke pushes me to the bed and spreads my legs. I moan

softly, gasping at each brush of his lips as he makes his way to my pussy.

My back arches off the bed when his tongue touches me. There.

"You're so responsive," Luke rasps, his words just as thrilling as his touch.

"Luke," I half-gasp, half-whine, not entirely sure what I'm asking for.

"I'm here, Addy. I couldn't stop if I wanted to."

His tongue delves into me, shooting ecstasy inside me and releasing it like a burst of fireworks. Then he's devouring me, long strokes up and down, pressing down on my clit each time he reaches it. Each primitive lick spits me into an impossibly higher level of pleasure. My hands shoot to his head, wanting him to stop. Needing him to keep going.

On the next pass he pulls back an inch, hot eyes boring into me as he wraps his lips around my clit and sucks. I almost buck off the bed as an orgasm rockets through me.

"Luke!" I cry, shuddering with each ripple that steals my breath. The sensations grip me, consume me, eat me alive.

"Mine," Luke growls, climbing over me.

With one swift move, his hot cock impales me, triggering another orgasm. An impossibly more powerful one.

I hold onto his shoulders for dear life as he pounds into me, the rhythm of his frenzied thrusts becoming the rhythm of my pleasure. I've never been so...full. So complete.

So in tune with another.

Luke roars as he comes, pumping over and over and over. He gives me everything he has. He claims me with jagged, out-of-control thrusts.

And when the final shudder rips through him, he collapses beside me and draws me in close.

As I curl into his heaving chest, I'm certain of what this is, of what we are.

It's everything I want. Luke is everything I seek.

And yes, I'm his.

I open my eyes to an unfamiliar, white-washed ceiling. It's day and scattered rays from the morning sun filter into the room through the open window.

I'm wrapped inside a bedspread that doesn't smell like mine. A man's hand is across my waist, the smell of sweat clinging to his skin. His breathing slips into my ear—slow, soft, his body rising with every inhalation. I glance in his direction, seeing his full frame sprawled out on the bed.

Luke.

The sight of the man who had made love to me last night brings a smile to my face. I can't see what Luke looks like when he's asleep because he's facing the other way, but I want to revel in his divinity forever.

He's spread out on the bed in his glorious abandon, spotless skin like refined gold. This same figure had cradled me last night, sending me to the gates of heaven. Luke had loved me with his body, his touch, every part of him. The connection I felt last night was out of this world, beautiful, the birth of something unforgettable.

A ripple of ecstasy shoots between my legs as I think about the sex. I squeeze my thighs to capture it, closing my eyes as it crescendos and falls back again. It's the magic of Luke Holland, a man who's made me feel like a woman again.

But he's a wolf. He's like me.

The thought steals my delight immediately, wiping the

smile off my face. I open my eyes and stare at sleeping Luke, remembering what he'd told me about my family.

It can't be true. My family would never hurt another so callously and deliberately.

But my stubborn conviction is as thin as a spindle, suscep- tible to being broken by a plausible truth. My brothers are violent. Lawrence is an unrepentant drunk. My father is consumed by an anger I can't comprehend. What's stopping them from barging into a pack and destroying it for no reason?

I get out of bed and find my clothes on the rug. Careful not to wake Luke, I tiptoe out of the room and dress in the sitting room. He's still sleeping when I open the front door and step out of his apartment.

The crisp morning air welcomes me as soon as I step outside. It's warm and cold at the same time, the morning sun peeping behind a cloud it's now taken as a cover. I walk briskly away from Luke's apartment, hoping to catch the morning bus that'll take me home.

Guilt compresses my heart with every step I take. Maybe I should have stayed in bed and waited for him to wake up. He's probably going to pretend he didn't tell me last night that my family members are pack killers. But I don't want to have that conversation with him. Not now. I have to deal with something else first.

"Hello," a voice from behind halts my walk, startling me.

I spin around, coming face to face with Luke's neighbor, the same man who told me Luke doesn't have friends, the man from 9A. He looks different today, as if he's shed some weight, his clothes drooping on his slender frame. The neighbor beams at me, the smile reaching his brown eyes.

"Hey," I answer, shifting back from him, suddenly aware that I have Luke's scent all over me.

Then it hits me that I'm not talking to a wolf. The neighbor is human. He can't possibly smell Luke on me.

Gosh! The fear of my brothers catching Luke's scent on my body has become a part of me, so much that it's my first thought when I saw the neighbor. How long am I going to hide the truth from my family? When will I have the guts to face them and tell them I'm seeing a wolf, the same wolf who claims they killed his family?

"I know you," the neighbor begins, his smile deepening. "You came looking for Luke a few days ago."

"Yeah, and you're the man who lives in 9A."

The neighbor nods, his gaze moving to the second floor where he lives. "I am. I bet Luke is in. Is he?"

"He is."

My eyes don't leave the neighbor's face. There's something off about him, like I can tell he's different from the rest of the humans. My suspicion heightens when I see the way he's grinning mischievously, and at the same time, scanning the area as though expecting danger to pop out of nowhere. What's he expecting? What's he up to?

"Okay, thank you," he replies, moving towards the stairs of the residential building.

"You're welcome." I turn on my heels and leave the area, crossing the road to flag down a cab.

A taxi soon appears, slowing to a stop beside me. As I bend to speak to the driver, my eyes catch Luke's neighbor. He's now on the second floor, standing in front of his apartment and staring at me from the railing.

The realization that I'm being watched sends a chill down my spine. Who the hell is he? Is he a wolf masking his identity with magic? I look away and tell the driver to take me to the bus station.

As I hop into the car, I take a quick glance at the building.

The neighbor is gone. He's not watching me, but a chill still rakes my body. It's almost as if he vanished into thin air but his creepy gaze has stayed behind, observing me.

The taxi takes me away from Luke and his scary neighbor. I wonder if the man from 9A is actually a friend of Luke's, someone he put on my tail. It's difficult to trust Luke now, after what he told me about himself. To think he'd deliberately hidden the truth from me, deceived me and taken me to bed while nursing hatred for my family. What if he's still lying to me and using a wolf to watch me, waiting for the time to unleash his vengeance on my pack?

It all makes sense now—the silent rage, the sudden interest in me, the grandma who doesn't even look like him. I'm so stupid not to have seen the warning signs, the red flags that Luke isn't who he claims to be. I was blinded by my desire, my burning passion for a man who made me complete.

And last night, I ran back into his arms and into his bed.

Whatever spell Luke is using on me, I need to save myself. He probably sees me as naive, a lonely woman who would cling to any man who shows her love.

Luke is wrong. I'm not naive.

I can decide what's best for me and right now, I want to know the truth.

I sneak into my room and shut the door behind me, waiting to pick up the sounds of my brothers in the big house. Nothing. The mansion is as silent as a graveyard.

Where is everyone? I move to my window and look outside. A few workers are in the garden, watering the flowers and weeding the area, but I don't see any signs of my brothers. The garden belonged to my mother. She loved planting flowers and named the garden after herself.

After her death, my father didn't abandon the garden. He continued to nurse it, the way my mother did. Five years later, it's still standing. His act reveals how much he loves the mate he lost.

If only he can let me love Luke the same way. It's impossible. He's going to kill me if he learns the truth.

I move away from the window and strip, going into the bathroom to have a good scrub. Luke's scent is drowned by the smell of my lavender soap, spinning with the bath water as it goes down the drain.

But thoughts of him occupy my mind, taunting me that I can't control what I feel. *He's going to always be in your head. You'll think about him every day, maybe blush a little, but he'll never leave your mind, no matter how hard you kick against it, no matter how angry you are with him.*

After my long shower, I go back to my room to get dressed. I wear a pair of black trousers first, then a black bra, standing in front of my mirror as I hook the cups on my breasts. Just staring at myself, I picture Luke touching me again, setting the pores of my skin ablaze. My mind is right. Luke has come to stay in my head forever.

I'm sliding my hands into the sleeves of my red top when I pick up the first sounds of my brothers. I hear Jake's voice first. He walks past my door, speaking to someone in a clear tone of displeasure.

"No, we're not going after Lanny's pack. He's a good friend!"

Someone grunts. "Oh, please." It's Lawrence. "He stole your woman. Isn't that enough reason to slit his throat?"

Their voices fade as they move further down the hall. Slipping the red top over my head, I open my door and step out of my room. Lawrence and Jake are still talking. They're in the foyer now. I wonder where Damian is.

"Jean married Lanny because she loves him. Who am I to choose the person she loves?" Jake answers.

"You're a pussy, Jake," Lawrence retorts. He laughs, a kooky laughter that resonates through the high ceilings. "You just can't stand up to Lanny, can you?"

"It's not that, Lawrence. I just have a bad feeling about this. We shouldn't do this."

"We should," a new voice says. It's Damian.

I creep towards the upper floor railing, ducking behind a shelf to avoid being seen. From here, I spot my brothers in the foyer, sitting on the padded armchairs there. Jake is by the window, twirling his watch on his wrist. Lawrence sits beside his younger brother, shaking a hip flask in one hand. Damian's the only one standing. His back faces me, awarding me a view of the large skull on his leather jacket.

"This isn't your business, Damian," Jake says. "Don't get involved."

Damian breaks into laughter. His laugh is a billion times more sinister than Lawrence's. Harsh, unpleasant, like fingers scraping a dry floorboard.

"I'm getting involved," he tells Jake, jabbing a finger at him. "You know why I need to be there when you slaughter Lanny's pack. That asshole sent his wolves to beat me up!"

I almost gasp, but intuitively, cover my mouth with a hand. Slaughter? Did Damian just say slaughter?

"He beat you up because you assaulted his wife, Jean!" Jake cries, slamming the wristwatch on the table beside him.

"I did it because of you, you ingrate!" Damian barks. "The woman ridiculed you by leaving you for Lanny."

"It wasn't your place to defend me! Jean made her choice."

"Lawrence is right," Damian spits. "You're a pussy."

Jake growls and tries to attack Damian, but Lawrence springs to his feet, stepping between them and stopping the fight before it even begins.

"Enough of this madness!" he bellows. "Are you going to fight and tear each other to shreds? Well, if you're going to do that, don't fucking spill blood on these chairs. I just got them."

Jake withdraws, his burning gaze still fixed on Damian. I can't see Damian's reaction but I know it's fiercer, madder. Lawrence watches them for a bit before he takes his seat back, chuckling.

"I guessed as much. You can't tear each other to pieces. You're still brothers."

He pauses to take a sip from his flask, then wipes his mouth and lets out a belch. Jake glares at him as if he's more insulting than Damian.

"And that's why, as brothers, we are going to storm Lanny's pack and kill every one of his wolves," Lawrence adds.

God! My brothers are truly killers! Tears gather in my eyes, the thought of their cruelty hitting me like a crushing boulder. Luke was right. And I didn't believe him!

"But Lawrence..." Jake begins but Lawrence stops in the rest of his words by raising a finger.

"Ah, no objections." Lawrence drops his hand. "Tonight, we feast on Lanny's pack. Those cheaters won't know what hit them."

"Are you done eavesdropping on your brothers?" someone says behind me.

I whirl around, fear clutching my heart as I see my father, his lofty figure towering over me. His eyes blaze with rage, his lips pressing into each other as he waits for me to answer.

He must have been standing behind me for a while. I'd been so preoccupied with the conversation that I didn't smell his presence. Even without that, I probably still wouldn't have known he's around. My father has a way of walking into a room without gaining attention. His strides are quick, silent, as if he hovers over the ground like a ghost.

I shoot to my feet, lips trembling as I think of the right words to say. But my father doesn't wait for my response. He grabs me by the arm and leads me to the foyer, his gray hair whipping backward with the swift steps he takes.

"Hello, boys." He lets go of my arm. "Say hi to your sister."

My brothers are now on their feet, surprised by our presence. I stand in the middle of the room, holding my arm where my father grabbed me. My heart begins a drum concert in my chest, pounding hard as fear envelops me, squeezing my insides. A part of me screams, *Run, Addy! Run!*

"Dad?" Lawrence talks first. "What's going on?"

Our father grins. He walks to one of the chairs and flops down on it. "Addy here wants to join in the conversation, isn't that right?"

I don't answer. My gaze stays on my father, intimidated by those inky eyes of his, those eyes that have seen the end of many packs. His hands are on the arms of the chair, hands stained with blood, the blood of the innocent.

He's no different from my brothers. Heck, he's the Alpha of the pack. My father's the mastermind behind these assassinations. He has my brothers under his thumb, controlling them, commanding them. They obey him like robots. They fear him like he's a god.

But he wasn't always like this. The father who raised me was quiet and caring, a man with listening ears. Growing up, I remember crawling into his bed at night when it rained and thundered. He'd let me curl up and then quietly take me back to my room after I fell asleep.

However, the man looking back at me is a stranger. He's a broken man who has cut ties with his other self. What happened to you, dad? Did the death of my mother turn you into a monster?

"No, she's not," Lawrence responds. "Go back into your room, Addy."

"I found her eavesdropping, Lawrence." Our father grins sideways. "She knows about the attack tonight."

"Is that true, Addy?" says Jake. "It's not what you think."

Damian hisses. "You don't have to explain shit to her, Jake. Whatever you heard is the truth, dear Addy. We're killing a whole pack tonight."

"Because we have to," Lawrence chips in. He approaches me, eyes studying my face as though I have something interesting plastered on it. "I know this may sound strange to you and you're probably shocked to hear this, but we're good people. We take out the bad people."

How dare he lie to my face? How can my own family look at me and feed me with lies?

"That's a lie!" I blurt out.

My outburst takes Lawrence by surprise. It's like a ripple effect, spreading across the room and slapping expressions of shock on these men's faces—well, except my father. He just looks at me, curiosity dancing in his eyes.

"What did you just say?" Lawrence asks, moving closer to me as if being near will change the fact that I just talked back to him.

I grit my teeth, raise my chin and repeat, "I said, that's a lie! I know what you all are. I know what you've been doing to other packs. I know the truth."

CHAPTER 13
LUKE

A ddy isn't returning her calls.

I rake my hands through my hair, frustrated that pacing my apartment hasn't made the time go any faster. Nor has it made her appear.

Surely after last night she realizes we can find a way to move forward...

I stare up at the bowel of the truck I'm lying under, trying to unwind my jaw. To distract myself, I grabbed my toolbox from the closet, and climbed under Jacqueline's truck, settling down to work on it. There's nothing wrong with the vehicle but I didn't want to spend hours thinking about Adeline and where she possibly is.

So far, it hasn't worked.

Someone kicks my leg as I lie under the truck, throwing my pulse into overdrive. I've never let anyone walk up to me without my knowledge.

"Hey, Luke."

I help myself out from under the vehicle, blinking as the morning sun hits my eyes. A figure stands before me and it takes me a few seconds to realize it's Jacqueline herself. My heart stops racing and disappointment stings me like an icy shower of rain. For a moment there, I thought it was Adeline.

"You don't look excited to see me." Jacqueline steps closer and I appreciate her figure blocking the rays of the morning sun.

I still find myself squinting up at her. "How are you, Jacqueline?"

She raises her chin once at the truck. "What are you doing?"

"Fixing your car."

"Did something happen to it?"

I rise to my feet, rubbing my dirty hands on my jeans. "Not really. Just checking it out."

"Well, someone's watching you."

I look at her. "What are you talking about?"

"Over there. At the railing. It's your neighbor," Jacqueline answers but she doesn't look behind her.

I do. Canopying my eyes with a hand to block the blinding sunlight, I glance back at the residential building. She's right. My neighbor, Ryan, is there. The one who lives in 9A. He's watching me with that creepy gaze of his and I wonder how long he's been standing there.

"What's with him?" Jacqueline asks, crossing her arms.

I return my attention to the truck. There are more pressing things on my mind, like where the fuck Addy is. "I don't know. He's just weird. And we don't really have much to do with each other."

"Let's stop talking about him, then. He gives me the chills." Jacqueline taps my shoulder, a smile curling the corners of her mouth. "How's Adeline?"

The question tugs at my heart. It's funny how you go from living your life, determined to be free of responsibility or relationships. Then next, someone like Addy walks into your life and there's nothing you won't do to hold onto it.

But if Jacqueline senses my worry, she won't leave until she's convinced me to give Adeline a call or go to her home. She has no idea Adeline's a wolf from the High Ridge Pack, the same people who killed my parents. Maybe if she knows, like the Blood Born pack, she won't hesitate to sentence Adeline to death.

"Adeline is fine." I beam at her, even as my worry threatens to wipe away the fake smile. "I'm going to be seeing her in a few hours."

Jacqueline returns the smile. She puts a hand on my shoulder while her eyes twinkle with tears. "It really is good seeing you happy, Luke. You light up when you talk about her. I haven't seen you this happy since..."

She chokes on the rest of her words, tears clouding her eyes now. Her anguish is raw, tugging at mine. I pull her to me, trying to wipe her tears at the same time.

"I know. It's okay, Jacqueline."

"I miss them too, you know," she sniffs. "They were my friends."

"It's impossible not to miss them."

We stay like that for a few seconds before Jacqueline pulls away and says she has to leave. I bid her goodbye and abandon my work on the truck. My neighbor is still there and his inquisitive eyes are enough to pull me back into my apartment. I get to my front door and mutter a greeting to him. He answers and says nothing again.

Where the hell is Addy? I ask myself as soon as I enter the apartment, stealing glances out of my window to catch her when she pulls up to the parking lot.

But no sign of her. Unease crawls over my skin. I can no longer escape the thought that's been prowling at the edge of my consciousness. The thought that something's happened to her.

My heart pounds in my chest at the thought of Adeline in trouble. The image of my woman being plunged into a situation that's way out of her control stirs my emotions. Her brothers! Have they found out about the two of us?

I move towards the cell phone I'd put on my drawer, waiting for her to call or text, and as my hand reaches for it, I freeze. Phoning Adeline will only make things worse if she is, in fact, in trouble. My call would only convince her brothers we have something going on.

Stop thinking about that! Adeline is fine. She's just tired.

Or she wants nothing to do with me...

The thought almost has me doubling over in pain. Is this the part where I let her go? The answer to the question is instant. Primal. A roar from the deepest part of my soul.

No!

It turns out once a selfish bastard, always a selfish bastard. I can't leave it like this with Addy. I want one last chance to make her happy.

I consider ringing the Blood Born pack but that would be like adding more coals to a furnace. The new pack isn't aware of my relationship with Adeline. If they found out about it, it would be the end of us. They want nothing to do with the High Ridge Pack and Adeline is a member. The daughter of the Alpha, in fact.

Besides, how would the new pack help me? Storm into High Ridge Pack's territory and save Adeline? I doubt it.

I'm left with one option. The Moonlit Bar. If there's one place I'll find her, it's in the confines of that bar, talking to her fellow mates. Although, seeing Adeline would definitely break my heart. What if she's there, talking to some other wolf?

What if she looks at me with cold disdain?

Shaking my head I grit my teeth. All those are questions I don't have an answer to. There's only one thing I know.

I'm in love with Adeline.

I grab my coat and walk out of my apartment. My neighbor is still there, still looking at the parking lot and now muttering to himself.

"Hey," I say, hurriedly closing my door so I won't have to continue a conversation with him.

"Hello, Luke," he finally talks, eyes settling on me. Then he looks back at the parking lot and continues muttering words I can't hear.

My neighbor's weird behavior is the least of my worries. Today, my phone is empty of Adeline's texts and calls. I'm beginning to miss her presence, her burning touch and her silvery voice in my head.

I decide not to take my car to Moonlit because I want to stay unnoticed, or rather, I want to sneak into the bar and find Adeline there, unaware of my presence.

The stuffy confines of the packed bar greet me as I stroll inside. All the regulars are there — except Adeline. Her usual seat is empty and there's no sign of her brothers either. It's impossible that Adeline had decided to stay at home without taking a bus to my place.

I go to the counter where her cousin, Carl, is pouring drinks. He beams at a customer before spotting me and then the smile vanishes. That reaction is enough to tell me he isn't happy seeing me here.

"You shouldn't be here," Carl grunts, reaching for a used mug. "Get out."

"Where's Adeline?" My tone is cold and I'm not going to show this man I'm scared of him — because I'm really not. I just want Adeline.

"I don't know." Carl's lips are quick to spill out the lie but his eyes give him away. He puts the mug on a shelf behind him and begins to wipe the surface of the counter with a napkin.

"You do," I sneer at him. "And I'm guessing you know who I am, too."

"Oh, please." Carl's groan is coated with mockery. "I do, but this is a bar filled with people like you. You do something funny and they'll tear you to shreds."

He's right and I'm more interested in walking out of here alive than revealing myself to the High Ridge Pack. I take a deep breath and try to subdue the rage inside me.

"Where's Adeline? That's all I want to know."

Carl leans forward. His voice drops to an almost inaudible whisper. "I know I can't make decisions for Addy and she seems to like you a lot. But you don't know what her family will do to you when they find out. So, just walk out of here and don't come back."

"No way. I want to see her."

"Dude, this is all the warning I can give. This isn't the right time. Just go."

In a few seconds, I understand why Carl's been trying to get me out of the bar. The smell of a familiar wolf hits my nose, stirring the memories of my encounter with him. A heavy slap lands on my shoulder, followed by a sinister scoff.

"There you are!" Lawrence says behind me.

I slowly turn. Adeline's brother is as scary as he has always been with his usual cruel grin playing across his lips. He's dressed in black, a biker jacket that hides his formidable figure and a pair of black jeans with spots of blood on them.

The sight of the blood alarms me. I don't know why I think it's Adeline's. Lawrence might be returning from a kill and forgot to wipe off the blood on him. Would he be so cruel to hurt his own sister?

"Hello, Lawrence," I greet him, maintaining the calm in my voice but deep down, I'm agitated, enraged, worried about Adeline.

"I'm surprised to see you here." Lawrence takes his seat. "Most of the new guys rarely come back."

I fix him a grin. "I'm not like the new guys."

Lawrence wags a finger at me. "I've always suspected that." Then he turns to his cousin. "Hey, Carl, whiskey?"

"Sure," Carl answers, but not without casting me an 'I told you' look before moving to the shelf behind him to pick a bottle of whiskey.

"So, why are you here? You like the bar?" Lawrence asks again.

I shrug. "It's not so bad."

"I see."

Carl is now pouring Lawrence his drink but something he does angers the wolf. Lawrence slams a fist on the counter, startling his cousin and making him spill some of the whiskey on the counter.

"I've always told you, Carl, that I don't want this tumbler. Bring me the other one!" Lawrence growls.

With a quivering hand, Carl takes away the glass, muttering an apology. The scene that just played out surprises me. Carl has always looked like a guy you don't mess with, but around Lawrence, he's a wimp like everyone else. I wonder if Lawrence is the Alpha of the pack, but I have no answer because I never asked Adeline. Her father is still alive, but has he surrendered his position to his intimidating son?

"They don't always listen," Lawrence says, massaging the bridge of his nose. "And I hate yelling at them. Do you have people who disobey your orders, Luke?"

Ha, he remembers my name, which is a bad sign because Lawrence must have a suspicion I'm here for his sister.

"No, I don't have any."

"They annoy me, you know?" Lawrence continues.

Carl is now back and he has a new tumbler, only slightly different from the former. So, what's the fuss about?

"Because I have to lead them, whether I like it or not." Adeline's brother watches me, maybe trying to gauge my reaction to his words. "This whole place, my family owns it. My dad is like this rich guy who's got a lot of people under him. When he's no more, I'll be the one in charge."

I know what he's doing. Lawrence wants to figure out who I am. He's scanning my face for any sign that I understand what his family is. They're wolves and Adeline's brother is trying to lure me into admitting I'm one, too.

"Oh." I feign ignorance. "What does your father do?"

Lawrence sighs and takes the whiskey Carl has stopped pouring. He brings the glass to his mouth and drinks, his eyes still watching me over the rim. When he sets the tumbler down, whiskey wets his upper lip and he wipes it off with the back of his hand. I notice bloodstains on his fingers.

"He's just a businessman." Lawrence grins. "What does your father do?"

If I wasn't convinced of the innocence of that question, I'd lose it right there, pulling out my claws and slashing at the wolf's face. If Lawrence knows who I am, then he's taunting me with that question.

But I grit my teeth to steady myself. My rage is screaming to burst out but I also bear the desire to live. The bar reeks of so many wolves and I can't possibly take them all out.

"My father is dead," I tell him. "But my mom lives in Washington. She's a fashion designer."

"Meh." Lawrence drinks from his glass again. "Women doing women stuff. That's why I don't want Adeline coming out of the house all the time. Fuck knows what goes on in their empty heads."

In addition to Lawrence's cruelty, he has no respect for

women. It's evident in how he controls his sister, like he has a leash on her and he's the only one capable of telling her what to do.

His words only fuel my temper. I can almost picture Adeline in the mansion right now, sitting alone in her bedroom because Lawrence has ordered her to stay in. Frustration coils through my muscles, impotent and toxic. If I'm hurt, there's nothing that I can do to save her.

"Well, my mom isn't a weakling. She's tough."

Lawrence chuckles. He stops talking for a while, focused on emptying his drink. After he's done, he pushes the tumbler to Carl, letting out a disgusting belch that hits his cousin in the face. The wolf let out a derisive laugh, ignoring the pained look on Carl's face.

He turns to face me. "She isn't coming here."

His statement is so random, I blink twice in confusion. "Huh?"

"Adeline isn't coming here," Lawrence clarifies. "I know you're here because of her but you're just wasting your time. She doesn't like you, okay? I'm sorry that it's coming from me."

I'm actually glad it's coming from him. Because then, I'm certain that the wolf is lying. Adeline may be hurting, but she has feelings for me. He's only trying to get me out of the bar.

"I didn't say I was here for your sister."

"Oh, please." Lawrence slaps me on the shoulder again. "I wasn't born yesterday. You're back here because you're hoping to see her. But Adeline is just like me, like her brothers. We don't really cling to feelings and I'm sure she doesn't want to have anything to do with you again. Do you want to know what she told me?"

"What?"

Lawrence leans forward and I can smell the whiskey on him. It almost overpowers the smell of his wolf.

"That you're just a fling. You're nothing more than that to her."

I don't say anything as I peer into his eyes where the lie twinkles with every blink. At this point, I'm convinced Lawrence had done something to Addy and doesn't want anyone looking for her. I'm tempted to tell him I'll go to the mansion and talk to Adeline myself.

But it would only cause Lawrence to fly off the handle. He'd take great pleasure in pinning me to the wall and ordering his wolves to tear me apart—every one of them—and then leave me to die.

"Okay." I flash him a grin. "Thanks for letting me know. I'll just go."

I turn around and head for the door of the bar. Lawrence doesn't stop me. Even his wolves who are watching me as I walk away do nothing as they remain in their seats.

As soon as I step out of Moonlit, I let out a breath of relief. It's a good thing to be out of the den of those wolves and back in the sun, where the afternoon air caresses my skin. I flag down a cab and go back to my apartment.

My next task is to find Adeline's scent but to do this, I have to shift. Shifting during the day is unwise of the risk of being seen by a human. But it would also alert the police. In this part of the world, the cops work for the High Ridge pack. The moment I was taken in, Lawrence and his family would be notified. Within hours I'd be dead.

I have to be careful and so, shifting at night is the best option. The dark will be my cover and the moonlight my guide.

The hours crawl like days. Each second is another without contact from Addy. They compound the knowledge that something's very, very wrong. As soon as it's safe to shift, I leave my apartment with no clothes on, hop over the railing and down to the parking lot. As my legs hit the ground, my body morphs into my wolf form and I dash into the inky night.

My first stop is Moonlit. The wolves are still there but I stay a considerable distance so they don't catch my scent. Lawrence's smell blends with the others and I know he's also at the bar. But amidst the jumble of wolf smells, I can't pick out Adeline's scent. She hasn't been here since I left the bar hours ago.

My concern grows with every step I take, checking out areas Adeline loves visiting. I even go to the park where the Strawberry Festival took place. Nothing. No sign of Adeline.

Forced to embrace the reality of Adeline being in trouble, I hurry to the Blood Born Pack where I know I'll find Fena. She lives in one of the cabins in the woods and is the only person I can talk to about Adeline.

Fena opens the door on the first thud of my paw on the porch. It's almost as if she's been waiting for me. I morph back to my human form, standing naked at the front of her cabin.

"Luke?" Fena says as soon as she sees me.

"I need your help."

She ushers me in, glancing outside for a few seconds before shutting the door behind her. She finds a blanket and wraps it around me.

"You shouldn't be walking all alone at night, not in these woods. The High Ridge wolves are scouring the forest again and it's best to stay indoors—"

"It's Adeline," I blurt before she's finished talking. "I think something bad has happened to her."

Fena pauses as she works around the room, closing the blinds. The woman looks at me for a long time. Then she sits on the only sofa in the room and motions to me to sit down too.

"Like what?"

"That's the problem." I use the edge of the blanket to swat

at an insect. "I don't know where she is. Adeline was supposed to be at my apartment hours ago but she didn't show up. I went to the bar where I first met her and she wasn't there. Then I met her brother."

"Which of her brothers?" Fena asks.

"Lawrence."

"That maniac," Fena hisses. "He's the most dangerous of them all, always out for blood. Did he say anything about Adeline?"

"Yes."

I tell her all that Lawrence told me and how I strongly believe Adeline would never call me a fling. Fena agrees with me. The High Ridge brothers are liars and they wield deception to their gain.

"Maybe Adeline is at home because she doesn't want to lead her brothers to you. I'm sure she's fine."

"No. I've got this feeling inside my bones that Adeline is in trouble."

"Okay." Fena tucks a strand of her hair behind her ear. "What do you want me to do?"

"I need your help finding Adeline. I don't know if I should involve the Blood Born pack."

"Wait, wait, hold up." Fena chuckles in derision, rising to her feet. "The Blood Born pack? That's impossible! You're not even a member yet and you want the pack to help you save a woman who is from the enemy pack?"

She's right but right now, my head is empty of better ideas. I desperately want to save Adeline. The thought of losing her buries me in anguish and my lungs close in as the pain envelopes me. I've never felt this way, never felt this fear and it makes me realize how much I love her.

"Then tell me what to do!" I get on my feet, too. "I can't just sit back and let Adeline's brothers hurt her.

Lawrence knows where she is, but he's never going to tell me."

"But you can't ask the Blood Born Pack to help you!" Fena snaps. She brushes her hair backward with her hands, breathing deeply. "Do you know what's going to happen if you tell them? They're going to kill Adeline. They're not going to care that she's the love of your life."

"Will you help me, then?" I search her face for an answer. "Will you help me save Adeline?"

Fena's expression is one that I can't read, but her answer is simple. Maybe she knows I have no one else to turn to.

"Fine, I'll help you, Luke. But we have to be careful. The Blood Born pack can't find out about this. Because if they do, the High Wolf is really going to be angry."

"The High Wolf?"

"Yes, the more powerful wolf who protects us. According to Arthur, I heard he's going to be coming to the woods one of these days to check on the Blood Borns. We really don't want him coming here and learning we saved a High Ridge wolf."

The idea of meeting this powerful wolf is intriguing. He appears to be a good man, a wolf who has given every lost and lonely soul somewhere to belong. And he's building an army, waiting to descend on the High Ridge Pack.

But saving Adeline is more important to me and I don't care whether the High Wolf likes it or not.

"Have you ever met this High Wolf?"

Fena shakes her head. "No one has. I don't know about Arthur though. But I've heard tales of the High Wolf that when he looks at you, you have no choice but to bow. He commands respect and most of the wolves fear him. His only worthy rival is the Alpha of High Ridge pack, Adeline's father. When he started this pack, he recruited wolves by hiring spies to watch them before deeming them fit to be a member of Blood Born."

"And has the High Wolf ever fallen in love?"

Fena is taken aback by my question. "What? How am I supposed to know that?"

I let the blanket fall and fix Fena with a determined look. "I'm a wolf who's tasted what true love is and I'm not going to back down because the High Wolf doesn't want it. I love Adeline and I'll do whatever it takes to save her."

CHAPTER 14

ADELINE

Darkness.

It surrounds me in the damp depth of this cellar. I crawl towards the door where a shaft of light slithers underneath but as soon as I near it, the chains holding me to the wall tighten around my wrists. They cut into my skin and a sharp pain courses through my hands.

I sit on the floor and think about what to do next. Nothing. There seems to be no escape in this hell where my brothers have placed me.

You're a wolf, Adeline. Break your binds, kick down the door and dash out of the room!

Except I'm a wolf who's been denied food, making me as useless as a sick human. I have no idea how long I've been down here, but since my brothers callously threw me in, there's been no sight of them. And no food. Pain makes my head spin and my vision blurs. All I know is it's been longer than my body can cope. Every now and then, my claws and fangs shoot out, desperate to tear into meat.

The need to eat overwhelms me. I've never been this hungry and this helpless, with no rescue in sight. My belly rumbles in protest and I drop to the ground. I soon give up trying to escape and I accept my fate. Weeping like a child, I curl up in the center of the room, waiting for death and the end of my anguish.

I think about Luke and the anguish multiplies. I left without talking. He probably assumes I never want to see him again. That I chose my family over him. The need to escape is just as much driven by the need to eat as it is to make things right between us.

I close my eyes and embrace the image of him in my head. It brings a smile to my face while my tears continue to fall. I imagine Luke is kissing me and getting rid of this biting ache in my tummy. His soft breath touches my skin and transports me into a sweet world of escape. His arms cradle me and I sense a moment of safety.

The door suddenly opens, interrupting my blissful moment. I canopy my eyes with a hand, trying to block out the blinding daylight flooding the room.

A figure towers over me. "Up!"

It's Damian. His harsh voice jolts me and I sit up, drawing my knees to my chest.

"How do you like your new room?" he snarls, moving further into the cellar and circling me menacingly.

"I..." I choke on my words because I'm too weak to even speak.

My lungs are parched up and my insides feel ready to erupt into flames. Werewolves have a high metabolism. We can't survive without food for the same time humans can.

Damian brings his face closer to mine. Insanity dwells in the pit of his eyes, burning, clawing for the surface. "Speak!"

"Please." My low voice reflects what I'm feeling inside— emptiness. "I need to eat."

I stretch a hand to clutch his leg but he slaps my hand away, forcing me to the ground. My stomach gnaws again, sending a barrage of aches to my head.

"You're going to stay here until you die, Addy." It isn't a joke. His tone reveals he's serious. "That's the price for confronting us."

"But I'm...I'm your sister." I can't even cry because my tears have all gone dry.

Damian chuckles. "A true sister won't talk back to her brothers. You're meant to shut up and not be heard. You got one taste of freedom and look what it did to you."

I reach for him again. His reaction is one I don't expect. Damian pins me to the ground, his hand gripping my neck while his knee digs into my thigh.

"Shut the hell up!"

"Enough, Damian," a voice booms in the doorway and from the corner of my eye, I see another figure.

Damian hastily rises to his feet. It's a relief when his hand leaves my neck. I turn on my side, coughing into the dusty floor of the cellar.

Lawrence is now in the room with us. He walks inside, his shoe searing prints into the dust. I can't look up to see him because raising my head worsened the throbbing pain, but his shoes come to stay in front of me.

"Sit up. I brought food."

If I wasn't locked up and starving, Lawrence's kind gesture would have been a clear message to run for my life. At this point, even the tiniest crumb is a feast in my eyes.

I struggle to sit up and realize Lawrence speaks the truth. In his hand, he holds a slab of meat and dangles it above me like I'm some dog he's about to feed.

"Take."

Lawrence drops the slab. I grab it before it touches the ground, digging my fangs into its juicy flesh. The taste explodes deliciously in my mouth, enveloping me in a cocoon of sheer strength.

I consume the meat in seconds, not sparing any part. I'm scared Lawrence will take it from me before I've had time to eat properly. It's a smart act because I don't know when next I'll get to feed.

Maybe it's my imagination, but a derisive chuckle comes from Lawrence. Shame stings my cheeks and I wonder how pathetic I must look.

I don't say anything and watch them, my gaze occasionally moving to the open door. If I can just make a move for it, would my chains snap under the little strength the meat has given me? Or maybe I should fool them with my tears and convince Lawrence to release me. They want to see me beg and that's what I'm going to do as long as it'll be my ticket out of here.

"Please, let me out," I plead, belying the rage I feel inside me.

"Poor Addy." Lawrence bends down. Our gazes level. "This isn't about what you want anymore. This is your new home and you won't be coming out of here for a long time."

My tears drop to the dusty floor. "I'm going to die here."

Lawrence straightens, moving away from me and standing beside Damian. A sinister smile plays across my other brother's lips as he tightens his fist, watching me. Is he going to try and hurt me again? I wanted to scream at Lawrence not to leave me here with Damian.

But my eldest brother has no plan to do that. He puts his hand on Damian's shoulder and says, "Come on, let's go."

"I need to see Luke!" The words are already out of me before I can stop myself.

My brothers pause, then turn around to look at me. Damian's expression of rage burns like a furnace.

But it's Lawrence's expression that scares me the most. An

amused smile floods his face and the glint in his icy stare has me wanting to retreat into myself. I don't though, keeping his gaze. Luke is fast becoming as essential as food.

He walks towards me again. "Luke? The new guy from the bar?"

I don't respond. The fear pounding in my heart seals my mouth and I pray my silence dissuades my brother from asking more questions.

It doesn't. Lawrence's moment of amusement expires, leaving his face to the grip of his anger. This is the first time since he stepped into the room that he's shown any sign of rage.

In the blink of an eye, his face is barely inches from mine. His heavy breath mingles with his fury, so hot it slams against my skin like a cremator. Sparks of indignation are visible in his eyes.

"When I fucking ask you a question, Addy, you reply!" he yells, my confidence turning feeble before him.

I lower my head to avoid staring at his face while every inch of me trembles, shivers, cowers.

Lawrence yanks my hair back, almost snapping my neck. I'm forced to look at him again, my teeth biting down on the torrent of pain coursing through my neck. His eyes have grown so dark they are like the core of an inky night, unable to be penetrated by light.

"Why do you want to speak to Luke?" my brother bellows.

"No reason!" Hot tears burn my cheeks. "We're just friends."

"Lawrence, let her go!"

My third brother, Jake, shoots into the room. He yanks Lawrence's grip from my hair and pushes him backward, away from me, before he can hurt me again. My oldest brother continues to glower at me. His look scorches me more than the agony overpowering my body.

"Stop doing that to her!" Jake growls.

But Lawrence just shoves him backward, so suddenly Jake almost rams into me.

"Stay out of this, Jake! She needs to be taught a lesson." Damian makes a show of coming closer to me but he's stopped by Lawrence stretching a hand in front of him.

"No one touches her but me," my oldest brother croaks. "I'm more interested in what's between her and this Luke."

I wipe my tears with my grimy hand. Now that Lawrence is several feet away and Jake is in the room to stop him from hurting me again, I embrace silence. It's best not to speak. Lawrence's curiosity will drive him to look for Luke.

The last thing I want is my brothers hunting down Luke. He's not a part of my pathetic situation, my war. This is between me and my brothers. I don't want him caught in their web of insanity.

Besides, trying to confront Luke about me would only reveal his identity to the High Ridge pack. I know Luke. He's no match for my brothers, for this cruel pack I've been calling family for years.

They've deceived me for a long time and now that I'm out of the darkness of my ignorance, I don't want my light to be Luke's downfall. I want him safe, away from this merciless world of mine.

He's been through enough. I'm not about to place him under another burden.

"I'm sure it's nothing." Jake glances at me and I see the kindness embedded in his gaze. At the same time, I can sense that he knows Luke and I are more than friends. He's trying to protect me.

As Lawrence opens his mouth to speak, another voice beats him to it. It's the low guttural voice of my father, coming from the upper floor of the home that's now my prison.

"Lawrence! Come here now!"

The blood drains from my oldest brother's face. He turns almost white, like he had just stumbled on a monster, far more dreadful than what he tries to be. For a moment, I'm convinced that he's turned into stone but he soon turns on his heel, bolting out of the room. Damian follows him out like an obedient dog.

An idea strikes me, one I hope will lead to my freedom. I'm sure my father has no idea I'm in this cellar. Maybe if I call out to him, the Alpha wolf will barge into the cellar and demand I be released.

"Dad!"

But my voice fails me. It's like trying to scream from the bottom of an ocean. My weakness buries me and I'm lost to its overwhelming grip.

"There's no point." Jake begins to walk out of the door, reaching for the doorknob to close the door behind him. "He's not going to hear you."

"Jake, please." I start crawling to the door but my chains stop me again. "Please, help me."

The look in his eyes tells me he wishes he could, but something is holding him back—Lawrence and my crazy brother, Damian, or maybe his loyalty to the pack.

"Bye, Addy."

Jake locks the door, sealing me into the depressing darkness of the cellar.

I don't even know when I begin to sob.

CHAPTER 15
LUKE

Something moves in the dark.

It's coming from the left side of the cabin, in the shadowy cluster of trees that lead into the heart of the woods. I bare my claws, moving to the window and focusing on the disturbance. The familiar smell of a wolf hits me and I know what to expect.

The sound grows nearer. Leaves jerk in their branches. A shadow leaps from the top of a tree and lands in the open space of the house. As soon as the figure touches the ground, I realize it's only Fena. I withdraw my claws and walk back to the couch I'd been sitting on.

She enters the cabin, dropping the hood of her sweatshirt. Her sour look tells me she bears bad news.

"What?"

"Those High Ridge wolves are getting closer. I need to tell Arthur. We should change camp."

I scoff. "There are dozens of you out there. Changing camps is like waving a sign over your head that tells the enemies what you are."

Fena flops down on the couch. "What are we supposed to

do? I'm scared, Luke. What if they break through our protection and kill everyone? You know what it means to lose your loved ones. I don't want to go through that nightmare again."

I take a deep breath and put a hand on Fena's shoulder. "You'll all be fine. Don't you have faith in this High Wolf? He's coming to your camp which means your protector is going to be with you even if the High Ridge wolves attack. Besides, I don't think they've got the balls to attack. A rival pack doesn't do that. They infiltrate the camp and pick out their weakest point."

Fena looks at me. Her sour expression morphs into one of pity. "Do you think that's what happened to your pack? They found your weakest point?"

I rub my nose bridge and exhale loudly. "I don't know. I think my father, if he were alive, would have an answer to that."

"Well, to hell with those greedy wolves!" Fena rises to her feet and pours herself a drink. "I'm not even scared of them."

I fold my arms and watch her. The fear coming from her fills the room and it rips a chuckle out of me. If Fena heard my derisive laugh, she doesn't act like it. She gulps her drink, closing her eyes as the liquid invigorates her.

"What did you find out?"

Fena turns to face me. For a moment, she appears clueless and then the meaning of my words hits her. She snaps her fingers and drops the cup in her hand on the table.

"Oh, that!"

Yeah, that, Fena. Not long ago, I sent her to the city to find out whatever she can about the High Ridge wolves, their locations and where they operate.

This is her way of figuring out where Adeline's brothers are keeping her. Fena has a credible source in Blood Born who is, in fact, a mole in the High Ridge pack. According to this source, Adeline's brothers haven't been at the mansion for some days. They saw no sign of Adeline, either.

If I wanted to make someone disappear without a trace, it would be unwise to keep such a person in their own home. Adeline's brothers are smart, especially Lawrence. The last place he'd lock his sister in is their family mansion. I'm desperate to find out the other possible places he could be using to keep her. She must be terrified.

Luke, there's one more thing you haven't thought about.

"No," I mutter to myself.

I don't even want to think about it. However, I've been pushing it to the back of my mind but it always surfaces, burying me in the depth of an encompassing depression.

What if Adeline's dead? What if I'm going to end up finding the dead body of the woman I love?

"I didn't find much." Fena's voice banishes the horrible thought.

I press my hands to the sides of my head. "Tell me."

"They have most of their homes in the southern part of the city," Fena answers. "I found out that Lawrence and Damian have been going to a particular home at Riverside."

I shoot to my feet, staring wide-eyed at Fena. "Lawrence? That's where he's keeping her."

Fena sees me reaching for my jacket. "Where are you going?"

I slip my hands into the sleeves. "Where's this place?"

"You're not going there, are you?" Fena chuckles. "Unbelievable! You're going to barge into a home of full High Ridge wolves just to save your woman."

I ignore her, heading for the door. "Where's this place, Fena? You said Riverside?"

"Stop it! You're only going to kill yourself." Fena blocks my way. She peers into my eyes, her glare boring into the core of reasoning. It's like she infuses my senses back into me.

"But I have no choice!" I shout, turning around to hide my

frustration from Fena. It burns so powerfully every deep breath I take does nothing to soothe it. "I have to save her, Fena. She's alone out there. She needs me."

"If you step out of this cabin, you're going out there to dig your grave," Fena tells me. "We have to come up with a plan."

I sit on the couch. "A plan? You and me? What can we possibly do to save Addy?"

"Go into the house and I'll be your lookout."

I brighten up at that idea. It would be great having another wolf watching the area for me while I try to look for Adeline. As a wolf, Fena would be able to pick out their scent from afar off and alert me.

"Are you going to howl when you catch their scent?" I ask her as we walk out of the cabin.

"No, silly. The wolves are going to know my howl isn't part of theirs. The alert word is Red Tomatoes."

"Red Tomatoes?"

Fena shrugs. "I love tomatoes."

We shift and race towards the road that leads to the regions where the High Ridge wolves operate.

It's not easy blending into the night and trying to avoid the enemies picking up our scent. But Fena has a thing for trees. She swings from one to the other, avoiding the grounds where the wolves creep. I use the trees as cover too, but I'm not as adept as she is.

We soon arrive at the house where Fena discovered Adeline's brothers visiting. It looks empty, a somewhat abandoned house with dingy windows and fading brown doors.

I smell the earth with my nose, trying to pick Adeline's scent. Nothing. Just the annoying scent of Lawrence and booze.

Does Lawrence have her buried somewhere, so far beneath the earth that her scent can't escape? Maybe in a box? In a basement?

In a coffin, Luke.

"No," I growl the words as a wolf.

Fena looks at me. *"What?"*

"Nothing. I don't think she's here."

"Then let's check the other houses."

"There are other houses? Why didn't you say that?"

Fena doesn't want to answer. She runs to the back of the house where two other similar houses stand. We walk with our noses in the ground and I finally catch Adeline's scent coming from the third house.

"She's here!"

Without waiting for Fena to speak, I race into the house. I'm so overwhelmed with the prospect of finding Adeline that I don't think of stumbling upon her brothers in the house.

To my luck, they aren't there. I continue to sniff the empty rooms until her smell leads me to the cellar. I shift into my human form and tug at the door.

"Adeline?" I cry, trying hard to remove the bolts on the door.

It surprisingly feels impossible to remove it, but I'm not giving up.

"Luke?" A weak voice responds from inside. "Is that you?"

"Adeline! I'm coming!"

Her voice multiplies my determination. As low and weak as it sounds, her response injects me with the strength of a hundred men and with one final tug at the bolt, the door flies open.

Adeline is in the center of the dark cellar, naked, bloody. She must have shifted several times to save herself because fur litters the ground. The binds make her wrists and legs bleed and she trembles like a child, curled up into a ball.

"Oh my God, Adeline." Tears threaten at the sight of her wounded body. I race to her, cradling her frail frame in my arms. "I'm so sorry."

She tries to talk but can barely open her mouth. Her parched body shivers as I help her to her feet.

"Let's get you out of here."

Carrying Adeline in my arms, I walk out of the cellar and into the empty living room of the house. Fena is at the door, still in her wolf form. Her nose soon flares up and her head swiftly turns in the direction where she must have caught a scent.

With blinding speed, she morphs into a human. "Red Tomatoes!"

I set Adeline on her feet but she's too weak to stand properly. Her knees buckle and she has to hold me for support.

"Hey, look at me." I put my hands on the sides of her face, trying to snap her groggy eyes to me. "Your brothers are back. We have to get out of here."

"They are?" Adeline speaks like she's in a trance. "Yeah, right. I can smell them."

"We have to hurry out of here."

Urgency thrumming through my veins, I scoop her up again and follow Fena out of the house. We race back to the first empty house in the area just as Adeline's brothers reach the place where they'd been keeping her.

A culmination of deep howls explodes from the house, informing us that the brothers have found out Adeline is missing. It rings through the night like a battle cry. The sound heightens my speed and my desire to protect Adeline from these monsters.

"Hold on tight," I say to Addy then morph into my wolf.

She curls up on my back, her fingers digging into my fur with surprising strength. We shoot through the forest as fast as our wolf strength can carry us. In no time, Fena, Adeline and I are back at the cabin, far from the piercing growls of the High Ridge wolves.

Fena locks the door behind us and I put Adeline down on

the couch. Her blood stains the material and I catch a wince on Fena's face.

"She's hurting," I groan in disbelief

"Whatever."

Fena goes to her cupboard to take a drink for the second time tonight. She pulls off the cap of the bottle with her teeth and before she swings it for a gulp, the female wolf asks. "Why isn't she healing?"

She's right. Wolves heal fast and Adeline's wounds should have gone by now. It worries me that her blood still drips and she seems to be in so much pain. I bend down beside the couch, placing a gentle hand on her.

"Food," she manages to croak.

"Oh, she needs to feed." I look at Fena. "Do you have anything?"

Fena nods and goes to another cupboard in the room. She pulls out a dead badger which appears to have been killed recently.

"Take it." She tosses it at me. "In the woods, you get to eat a lot of animals."

I take the badger to Adeline's mouth and watch her fangs sink into the flesh of the animal. She feeds, groaning as the act returns her energy. The wounds on her body respond to the food too, closing up and losing their angry red inflammation.

After Adeline has had enough to eat, she takes her mouth away from the badger and draws a long breath. The corners of her mouth are lined with blood from the animal and she curls her tongue over her fangs.

"You should rest," I tell Adeline. My hand strokes her now smooth flesh.

It's a relief to have her back. Though she's wounded and looks like she's trudged through a storm that left her broken and bruised, it's calming to sense her skin against mine again, redeeming me of my fear.

Adeline isn't six feet underground. She's sleeping on Fena's couch, her beautiful eyes staring back at me while a small smile plays across her lips. The realization that she's safe now brings tears to my eyes again. This time, they drop because I can finally breathe again.

She's my woman, the heartbeat that keeps my heart going. I don't want to think about what I would have done if Adeline had died. That's a world of misery and anguish and endless night that I can't even conceive.

I stop stroking her skin and wipe a lock of her hair from her face. As my hand moves away from her hair, my fingers brush against her lips and, for the first time, I sense how dry they are. She needs water. Rest.

But at the same time, I want to reach forward and pull them into my mouth. God! I've missed kissing her! I miss tasting her like she's the sweetest thing in my world while my hands press the small of her back. I miss getting lost in the burning sensation of savoring her mouth, taking her completely and burying myself in the feeling.

"I'll be at the camp if you need me." Fena is already walking out the door. "You know the way there, don't you, Luke?"

"I do."

"We are making preparations for the arrival of the High Wolf," Fena adds.

My tone is a little harsh when I respond. "Okay. Bye, Fena."

I can't wait to be alone with Adeline. Fena must have figured that out because she hurries out of the cabin, locking the door behind her.

Adeline turns on her side, fully facing me now. Her gaze continues to warm my body and it's relieving to see the glow returning to them. I bring my face closer to hers and kiss her softly.

"I missed you."

"Me too."

I sit beside her and put my arms around her as she sits up. She reeks of the dampness of the cellar which means they've kept her there for days. I fight the urge to return to the house and rip Lawrence's heart out for laying a finger on my woman.

"I'm sorry for everything, Luke."

Her apology catches me off guard. Sorry for what? When tears drop from her eyes again, I stop them with my lips, planting kisses on the spots that glisten.

"Sorry? What are you apologizing for, Adeline?"

"For making you go through the trouble of looking for me." Her shoulders tremble again and grief overwhelms her face. "If my brothers hadn't tied me up and..."

The rest of her words die because I reach forward again and kiss her. This time, it lasts longer. A burst of ecstasy surges through my body and instead of Adeline trembling, it's my body that quivers in response, the hunger to explore her hitting me like a fiery sea.

When I pull away, Adeline beams. Her tears have stopped flowing and she appears relaxed, as if the kiss has driven away whatever piercing cold of fear she had inside her.

"Adeline, I know you didn't cause this. I always suspected the women of your pack didn't have much involvement in this mess."

Adeline brushes a strand of her hair from her face and sniffles aloud. "But they're my family."

"You don't have to be with them." I squeeze her hand and make sure my gaze doesn't leave her face. "You've seen what you mean to them. They don't love you. A loving family would never have done that to you."

"I have no idea when they got so evil." Adeline appears to rack her brain as though remembering the very point in her life when her family became cruel would wipe the reality of what they truly are.

I rub a thumb over a smear on her cheek. "It doesn't matter. They chose to be heartless and destroyed so many lives. It's not your fault."

"My dad." Adeline's voice fades. She starts crying again. "I don't know what changed him. I'm guessing it's my mother's death."

I leave her side to grab a bottle of beer from Fena's refrigerator. Adeline is still talking about her father as I pour drinks for the two of us. She talks about how he'd been so broken after her mother's death and the unfortunate incident must have driven him nuts.

"I don't think you should talk about your family now, Adeline." I hand her a cup. "The important thing is that you're safe and your brothers can't touch you again."

She sips her beer and closes her eyes, suddenly looking drowsy. Resting her head on my shoulder, she sighs. "You're right. I can never be a part of the High Ridge pack again."

CHAPTER 16

ADELINE

S omeone walks into my room.

I hear the footsteps first and then the sound of chains rattling on the wooden floor. My brothers are back. Their stench floods my nose and the rough hands of Lawrence yank me from the comfort of my bed, pulling me back into the cellar, where I'll be chained for all eternity.

"No!" I scream, sitting up instantly, kicking the sheets away from me.

"Hey, hey, it's me!"

Strong arms close around me, a familiar, comforting smell seeps into my mind, and when I look up to see who's holding me, Luke's soothing smile greets me.

I'd been dreaming, plunged into a nightmare of being captured by my brothers again. Waking up to realize I truly had been taken makes me shudder.

"Oh, thank God." I collapse in Luke's arms. "Thank God you're here."

He kisses me tenderly on the head. "I'm never going to leave you."

The room in the cabin where Luke had tucked me in last

night is brightly lit and it takes me a few seconds to note it's already morning. Sunlight floods the room through the sash window, the occasional chirping of birds in the trees also filtering in.

"I made breakfast."

Luke begins to pull away but I hug him tighter. "Don't leave me, please. I'm scared."

He doesn't speak again. He just sits with me. His touch is tender and every kiss on my forehead speaks a language of affection.

I close my eyes and imagine our lives are perfect, free of my family's troubles and his heartbreaking past. I picture what it would be like waking up beside him every morning or walking with him along the shore of an ocean.

It's a beautiful life, one I hope that I'll have one day. We don't deserve what's been hitting us lately. We're only two wolves in love.

"Luke?" I open my eyes and raise my head to look at him. "Do you promise to stay with me forever?"

His intense gaze gives me an answer before he even opens his mouth to speak. "Yes. I love you, Adeline. There's no doubting that."

Breaking into a smile that fully stretches my mouth, I move my lips to his and kiss him. Luke responds, warming my insides with his unique flavor of heat.

His movements are sweet and fiery at the same time. When his hands make contact with my skin, it's like I've been dunked into a furnace of pleasure, my body itching for what's coming.

I can't deny Luke's kiss is transforming me. I was a being of fear but now, I'm riding on clouds of bliss. The million voices of my brothers in my head fade and for the first time since I left the cabin, my head is clear. Free.

Luke breaks the kiss to move his lips to my jaw and down

my neck. I close my eyes, welcoming all that he does. His lips find my earlobe and he tugs at it with his teeth, sending hot shivers dancing over my skin.

As he kisses me, I rub his back with my hands. Through the fabric of his shirt, I feel the ripple of muscle and sinew, sense the movement of his body, the rapid swelling of his chest as he continues to explore me. His breath is hot against my skin and the musky scent of his excitement fills my nostrils.

This alone is enough to make my legs tingle. A hot sensation travels up my thighs and settles in my groin. Adrenaline floods the floor of my abdomen and as Luke tugs off my nightdress. I know it's a matter of time before my delight turns into a chorale of moans.

Luke pushes me to the bed gently. His big body stays on top of me while my legs wrap around his waist. As he drops his head to my breast, I arch my back and let out a soft moan.

The tip of his tongue fondles my nipple as his thumb squeezes the other one. All I can do is run my fingers through his hair as the pleasure consumes me. Luke's groans are short, almost strained, yet pleasing to the ears. It's more of a turn on to know he enjoys what he's doing to me.

His lips leave my bare breasts, then he whispers into my ears, "You're beautiful, Adeline."

I slide a hand into his pants and find his already hardened cock. When I touch it, Luke's reverberating groan lingers in his throat as his eyes flare with delicious heat. Still peering into his gorgeous eyes, I stroke him softly.

His entire body shakes in reply and as I heighten the sensation but gripping just a little tighter, his cock throbs, undeniably eager to be inside of me. But not yet. I want to hear Luke call my name and revel in the hunger in his voice.

"Yes." His soft breath grazes my face.

Luke grits his teeth and swallows the groan he's about to

release. But he can't fight it and when he finally blurts out my name, I push him onto his back, taking the top position now.

He puts his hands on my waist and waits, panting, as I slip his cock into me. We both throw our heads back, our moans tangling.

"Wait," Luke growls. His penis slips out of me as he sits up straight and pulls his pants down properly, so they now circle his ankles.

When he enters me again, my body is almost trembling with anticipation. I want him in me. I want to feel complete in only the way he can. As his hot length slides inside, stretching me, filling me, I have to clamp my hand over my mouth to stifle my moan.

Luke holds my hips while I ride him, gently at first, but soon, it's not enough. I move faster as his hands grip, fingers digging into my skin, helping me find a thrilling, slapping rhythm. My hair brushes my bare back as I curve my spine, grinding my ass on his groin each time we connect.

A kaleidoscope of sensations collide and explode inside me. It's like being stuck in a whirlpool of elation, turning and turning as deep down, an ocean of joy overflows.

My legs throb as the thrill deepens. Luke has his eyes closed, sexy grunts reverberating deep in his chest. When I bring my mouth forward to kiss him, the touch is passionate and sets me on fire again.

With a sudden twist, keeping our bodies intimately connected, Luke sets me down on my back and takes control again. He places my hands above my head, pinning my wrists to the bed. With a single thrust, my butt presses deeper into the mattress, parting a way for his dick to explore me better.

I cry out. Every thrust is heaven. Every kiss is paradise. It's pure, tender perfection. His lips aren't moving but it's like they're speaking to me, telling me he loves me, forever and ever.

The physical combustion, the emotional totality, is overwhelming. Yet, it's everything. The truth spills tears from my eyes. I can't stop myself, not when this is everything I want. Luke tries to pull away, thinking he's hurting me, I put my arms around his neck and hold on tightly.

"I love you, Luke."

My words send him over the edge. His body jerks above me, his dick swelling impossibly more in the confines of my walls. When he shoots his come inside me, it's a warm sensation of ecstasy that I'm honored to feel. It triggers my own welcome release, the pleasure that had been pooling like molten lava exploding like a supernova. Stars are born and destroyed behind my eyelids, the cosmos touches me and I touch it. Yet all I can feel is Luke. Heating my heart. Caressing my soul.

I'm not sure how many lightyears pass before I open my eyes, but the sensation of Luke pulling away has me returning to blissful reality.

"What's wrong?" he asks as he rolls away from me.

I put my head on his chest and hear his throbbing heartbeat, drawing the scent of sweat and passion deep into my lungs. It's what I want to experience every day of my life.

Nuzzling his still-hot skin, I don't let any more reality intrude on this moment. "Nothing. I'm just happy we're together."

It's whether it can stay that way that we'll have to face the moment this intimate bubble bursts.

CHAPTER 17
LUKE

"What's your plan?"

The question comes from Fena. She's sitting on the front verandah of the cabin, smoking. Every time she takes a long drag of her cigarette, she puffs into the starry night, making almost flawless rings of smoke.

It's been a full day since Adeline was rescued from her brothers and I've spent the time caring for her, sleeping with her, making love to her. It's been bittersweet. It's a taste of what life could be like for us. Yet her constant jumpiness, the way she clings to me like I'm a lifeline, is a reminder of what she's been through.

It's a reminder of what waits for us.

Fena, on the other hand, has spent her time with the other wolves in the Blood Born pack. She told her friends not to come visit her cabin because she didn't want them to see Adeline.

Honestly, I'm glad. I don't have the strength to explain to Arthur that Adeline isn't like her brothers.

"I don't know." I sit beside her, watching as she makes another ring. It lingers in the air for a few seconds and then fades. "Do you always do that?"

Fena grins. "Yep."

I look away to stare at the woods before us. Darkness blankets the area but it's not enough to kill the light from the full moon. Humans assume all werewolves should be out tonight, shifting and howling because the moon is what makes us what we are.

But that isn't entirely true. We have the ability to shift anytime we want, full moon or not. It's just a myth humans have passed down from generation to generation to keep people indoors during full moon and to make shifters appear vulnerable to nature.

During a full moon, a shifter's strength doubles and that's the only effect I know the night light has on us. Just sitting with Fena in front of the house, I can sense a fiercer amount of strength coursing through my body, like I'm on steroids and the moonlight is my drug.

"Where is she?" Fena flicks her half-burnt cigarette so that it drops on the grass. She squashes it with her boot.

I glance behind me as if I can see Adeline in her room from here. But the door of the cabin greets me with its wood chipping in several places. I face Fena. Her curved eyebrow tells me she's waiting for an answer.

"Asleep. She's really troubled, Fena. I don't know how to help her."

Fena scoffs. "The sex didn't work?"

My cheeks burn as I break into a grin. "Ah..."

"I'm not dumb. I've been home three times today and each time, you were in bed with her." Fena slaps my shoulder and squeezes it roughly. "Just know you're not leaving here without cleaning my sheets."

"Aye, aye, captain!" I tease.

"So, what's up with her, exactly?"

"Nightmares. She's finding it hard to sleep."

"It'll go away."

Fena doesn't sound concerned about Adeline's nightmare. It's almost as if she's dismissing it. "Well, that was blunt."

Fena tilts her head to look at me. "It's the truth."

"It's Adeline." I breathe deeply. "I should worry about her."

Fena plays with her fingers now. "I don't usually tell people this story but what's the point of keeping it to myself?"

I wait for her to continue. Most of the time, when people start their statement that way, they're about to divulge a significant secret—and it would be wise not to interrupt them.

Fena stares out into the forest, her eyes losing focus. "After my pack was slaughtered by the High Ridge wolves, they took some of us prisoners. I was one of them. Adeline's pack members kept us in one of their large homes a few miles from here. It's how I know some of their homes where they hang out and keep people."

I follow Fena's line of sight, hearing the pain she's trying to keep under control. The night breeze rustles the leaves of the trees. I can smell the rain in the air and see streaks of lightning in the sky. In front of us, dead leaves move in several directions while night creatures hurry into their holes to avoid the impending rain.

It's rather interesting how a calm night can suddenly turn turbulent. It's clear a storm is coming. Just like my life, it had been calm until the High Ridge wolves came as a cruel storm.

"They kept us in their homes for days and killed us like animals. Some of the wolves forced themselves on the female wolves. It's horrifying to even remember." Fena sniffles and wrinkles her nose with her hand. "I could have been killed too but one of Adeline's brothers kept me alive. He was impressed by how unflinching I was when the wolves came to terrorize us."

"Which of her brothers?"

"Jake."

I wasn't really expecting her to say Lawrence. That wolf will never bat an eye before ripping out the innards of another person.

"Then I fell in love with him."

I look at Fena as though she just grew horns. In love? With a High Ridge wolf?

Fena scoffs. "Don't judge me. You're the last person who should be doing that."

I shake my head. "I'm not. Just surprised. You were his prisoner. How did you fall for him?"

Fena stomps on the cigarette again. It's now a black smear of ash on the grass. The wind continues to blow, picking up things in its path. I think about telling Fena we should go inside but again, I don't want to interrupt her story.

She flicks me a glance. "Ever heard of Stockholm Syndrome?"

Who's never heard of Stockholm Syndrome? Maybe people who don't find it attractive falling for one's captor.

"Did he treat you right?"

"Yes. Jake was very nice to me. He was different from the rest."

"But he didn't let you out of the house."

Fena leans backward, supporting her posture with her hands on the floor of the verandah. "You don't understand. I'd been held as their prisoner for months and then someone showed up, acted all nice to me, smiled at me and even fed me. What did you expect? I was in pain and I desperately wanted to feel loved."

"Still surprising. I don't think I could have done that."

Fena chuckles. "You're already doing it."

I knit my eyebrows in confusion. "How so?"

"We are both attracted to people who are keeping us

captive. Adeline doesn't have to put you in chains to do this. Her problems are holding you down. They're stopping you from soaring. But you love feeling that way. You love taking her problems and making them yours."

Fena's words sting. I'm annoyed that she's calling Adeline my captor. No, Adeline isn't that. In fact, she's my freedom, the person who has broken my chains.

I haven't felt this happy since my pack's murder. Adeline's presence is the bubble of light my heart is wrapped in. I've never felt so peaceful since I came to this city. Adeline's love is the blissful silence healing my soul. How dare Fena say she's my captor?"

"That's not true," I croak. "Adeline is the best thing that's ever happened to me. This is different, Fena. I love her and I'm not her prisoner."

"She's chaining you to her problems, Luke. Can't you see it?"

My jaw stiffens. "If you're saying I should forget about Adeline and stop loving her, that's not possible, Fena. I'll love Adeline until my last breath."

Fena rises to her feet, dusting the dust off her pants with her hands. "Whatever. As for me, I had to learn to stop loving Jake. His family is trouble. I don't want to be caught in the middle of anything."

But Adeline isn't Jake. She's different from her brothers. That's why my love for her will continue to burn.

"It's pointless trying to convince me."

I rise to my feet too. The wind is getting wilder and it would be foolish sitting on the verandah and letting it spit dust in our eyes.

"I'm thinking about my next plan," I add. "I'm not sure of what to do yet, but I want Adeline's brothers to pay for what they did to her."

We're now inside, but we keep our voices low not to awaken Adeline. Besides, I don't want her to hear me talk about her brothers. Their names alone are enough to trigger her painful memories.

"If you choose to fight back, the Blood Born pack might help you."

I frown at her. "Isn't that what we're trying to avoid? The pack doesn't need to know about Adeline's capture and how I saved her. You said it yourself. They're going to hate me."

Fena rolls her eyes. "We don't have to tell them that. All we need to say is that the High Ridge wolves attacked us and we feel it's time to fight back."

"Except they outnumber us," I point out. "We'll be no match for them if we fight back now. I don't want more death on my conscience. It's the last thing I want for this pack that has accepted me. But I'm not going to run. I'm not going to show Adeline's brothers I'm a coward. This is my fight, my burden. I'll do this myself."

Fena addresses me with pity in her eyes. "You don't want to set yourself free, do you?"

Before I can answer, Adeline walks into the room. Fena sees her first because she's facing the direction of the bedroom.

"Hello, Adeline," Fena smiles at her, signaling with her eyes that I should look behind me,

I turn my head and the sight of Adeline pulls a sharp breath out of me. She's wearing Fena's sweatshirt which isn't long enough to cover her smooth curvy thighs, so sexy my cock tightens. Her messy hair falls down her shoulders, urging me to reach forward and snake my fingers through it, Fena or no Fena. My lips would find hers again and I suppress the groan of pleasure at just the thought of caressing her beautiful body.

"Hello, guys," Adeline answers, a delightful smile grazing her lips.

I take a deep breath and cross the room to her. She inches her face close to mine so I can peck her on the cheek.

"How are you feeling?"

"Fine," she says, even though she's far from that. "I came out to make tea. Do you guys want some?"

"Sure." I brush a strand of her hair from her face. "I don't mind."

"What about you, Fena?"

The female wolf's grin stretches to the corners of her mouth. "Yeah, sure. Thanks, Adeline."

Adeline walks into the kitchen to make tea for us all. Fena hurries to my side and whispers to me. "Do you want to tell her about your plan?"

"No, of course not. Adeline is going to object."

"But you can't go behind her back to fight her brothers," Fena insists.

Adeline pokes her head out of the kitchen. "Sugar, Fena?"

Fena beams. "No sugar."

Adeline disappears into the kitchen again. I'm worried our whisperings will raise Adeline's suspicion that we're saying something we don't want her to hear. But it's best if she doesn't. Although this is her fight, I'm about to make it mine.

I glare at Fena. "She doesn't have to know so please, keep this to yourself."

"You're crazy to think I'll let you go on that suicide mission," Fena huffs. She glances at the doorway to the kitchen. "Look, I'll gather some of my friends in the pack. We'll help you. You don't have to worry about doing this on your own."

Adeline returns with a tray of tea. She sets it down on the table in the sitting room and points to a red teacup. "That's yours, Fena."

Fena bends to take the cup. She sips a little from the tea and nods. "Perfect, Adeline."

"You're welcome. I hope you don't mind. I rummaged through the kitchen."

Fena thanks her with a soft, knowing smile. "It's okay."

Then Adeline looks at me, her teacup in hand. "I have a confession to make."

I'm just reaching for my tea. "What's that?"

"I overheard your discussion," Adeline replies.

I cut my gaze to Fena. She avoids looking at me by bringing the cup to her mouth and taking a rather long sip.

"You weren't supposed to hear that."

Adeline smiles. "It's okay, Luke. I get it."

The teacup warms my palm. "And you're not going to stop me?"

Adeline drinks from her tea again. "No, honestly. I won't stop you. But Fena is right. My pack outnumbers the new pack. I haven't met the Blood Born Pack or seen how many wolves they have but I've seen mine and we breed like there's no end of the world."

"I'm not going to sit back and let your brothers get away with what they did." Anger simmers low in my gut. "I'm going to make them pay and I don't care how many wolves I have to face."

Fena sits on the couch, placing one leg over the other. "He's so obstinate, Adeline. How did you even fall for him?"

Adeline chuckles. "Luke has got a good heart, but his good heart is going to be the death of him." She puts a hand on my chest. "If not for yourself but for me, don't go after my brothers alone."

I take her hand and squeeze it gently. "I refuse to let them win."

"Then if you must fight them, I'll fight alongside you."

CHAPTER 18

ADELINE

"That's insane," is the first thing Luke blurts out.

He drops the tea and regards me as though I just talked about leaping from the Empire State building. Honestly, I don't understand his rage. He's doing this for me, isn't he? Why does he not want me to fight this war with him?

"You'll need me," I insist and Luke hisses, turning his back to me. "I know everything there is to know about my brothers. I'll be of great help to you."

"No, you're not fighting!" Luke snaps, facing me again. "I told you I'll fix this. You don't have to get involved."

His words baffle me. Luke's flashing eyes tell me he's angry. I don't know why he's overprotective all of a sudden. It's the same reason I fled from my brothers.

Then it hits me. Maybe Luke isn't doing this for me after all. When we first met, I was a way for him to infiltrate my pack and get his revenge. What if I'm still that conduit of vengeance? He's going to spew me out like a bland gum.

"Aren't you doing this because of me?" I ask him, trying to keep my voice strong even as my heart constricts painfully. "Or are you doing it for yourself? Has this been your plan all along? To use me and dump me when it comes to the real deal?"

"What? No!" Luke looks around wildly, like he's just been cornered, then storms out of the room, his heavy footsteps echoing throughout the cabin. I glance at Fena, expecting her to tell me I said something wrong.

She raises her shoulders and drops them again. "I don't know what's gotten into him."

I sit down beside the female wolf, drawing my hands up my face. "Oh, God." Our enemy blood is already coming between us.

"Give him time," Fena says. "He'll come around."

I face her. "You agree that I should fight, too?"

"Why not? You're a wolf, not a weakling."

"Then why is he behaving like it's the end of the world?"

Fena looks away and doesn't speak for seconds. "Because he loves you and doesn't want to see you get hurt," she says softly.

Maybe she's right. The possibility of Luke objecting to my involvement because he loves me warms my heart. At the same time, it could be ego or pure need for vengeance that Luke deems himself the only person capable of bringing my brothers down. I'm not going to sit back and let him get hurt, especially when I'm the cause of this.

"What do you think I should do? I'm not going to let him harm himself."

"It's not like he's a weak wolf," Fena chuckles but the glare I give her buries the laughter. "Look, you're right. You should fight alongside him but it's just going to be the two of you. It's the same thing, a suicide mission. You need other wolves who can help you."

"You talked about telling some of your friends to help us. Is that going to be possible?"

Fena rises to her feet. "Yes but we can also do something else for you."

"What's that?"

"Hide you so your brothers don't ever pick up your scent." Fena turns to face me, her face somber. "Forget this mission and join us."

I shoot to my feet. Join the Blood Borns? I'm not sure Luke would approve of that, and at the same time, I don't know what I'm getting into renouncing my pack and joining another. Is there some ancient repercussion for pack renegades?

"Uh, I...I don't know what to say. I guess I'll think about that."

Fena cocks an eyebrow at me. "So, you won't fight your brothers?"

"If Luke fights them, I will. But maybe you're right. Maybe we should forget about this and join the pack. Luke's scent is all over the cellar. I'm sure my brothers are looking for him now."

Fena slaps me on the shoulder. "Whatever you choose to do, remember you've got a future too. Don't throw it away."

With that, the female wolf walks out of the cabin, leaving me to the heartbreaking reality of Luke's stubbornness.

CHAPTER 19
LUKE

I step into the rain.

The icy torrent washes over me, surprisingly calming me. As shifters, we don't get affected by cold or heat. Our bodies are known to withstand any weather and so the heavy rain has nothing on me. I just want it to pour on me and hopefully subdue this anger boiling inside me.

Fight alongside me? Hell no! I almost lost Adeline. I'm not losing her again. Lawrence and his brothers will kill her when they get a hold of her. There will be no cellar this time and no chain holding her to the wall. Being starved would be the least of Adeline's problems because they won't even spare her to remember what it means to be hungry.

But she won't listen. Adeline must think she's protecting me by trying to get involved. I'm the one protecting her. This is bigger than she thinks, more dangerous than she feels.

"Stop being a selfish bigot, Luke," Fena speaks behind me.

I wheel around to see her standing on the verandah, her hands in the pockets of her jeans.

"Stay out of this, Fena," I growl.

The rain pelts me now, threatening to trickle into my ears.

Shifters may be resistant to unfavorable weather but not the annoying feeling of having water in our eardrums. So I head back to the verandah, dripping all over the floor.

"I should stay out of this?" Fena demands. "Please, like you can last one second without Adeline!"

I flash her a look. "What do you mean?"

"She's going to get real angry with you, Luke, because of your attitude, and instead of losing her to the cold hands of death, you're going to lose her by watching her walk out of your life."

The reality of making Adeline doubt my love for her strikes me now. She thinks I'm going after her pack because it's always been my goal and not because I'm angry they hurt her.

I don't say anything to Fena but turn around and enter the cabin. Adeline is sitting on the couch now, her face buried in her palms. Her heartbreak touches me and I don't even have to see it in her eyes or on her face. It's there, in the way her shoulders have dropped and her spirit is fracturing.

Without making a sound, I walk up to her, gently go on one knee and hold her by the wrists. Adeline is startled at first but then her teary eyes recognize me and she breaks into a sad smile.

"Luke, I'm sorry, I didn't mean..."

I don't let her finish. "It's okay. I said those things because I don't want to lose you. I want to be by your side forever."

Adeline rubs her runny nose but I don't mind holding that hand again. She's everything I want and even in her weakest moment, I want to be her strength. In her lowest moment, I want to be her highest point.

Tears roll down her cheeks now. "Me too."

I kiss her tears and cause her to laugh now. "I can't imagine a life without you."

"Me too. My life would be one dark tunnel."

I clutch her hand tighter. "Then let's run away together, me and you, right now."

Adeline's eyes widen. She can't believe what she's hearing and I expected this kind of reaction. I only thought about this a few seconds ago when I walked into the cabin.

Why not run away with Adeline? This is about me and her, not anyone else, not her brothers. We don't have to fight them. We don't have to join a new pack to exact revenge on them. This is our future and nothing is going to stop us from building it together.

"Come with me, Adeline." I lift her hands gently and kiss the back of them. "Let's make this about us."

"What about revenge?" Adeline searches my face for an answer. "Don't you want to make them pay?"

"I choose you, not my rage, not my vengeance. Don't you know how much I love you, Adeline? I'm willing to sacrifice everything. You're mine and I'm never going to lose you."

My words bring more tears to her eyes. She sniffles and begins to cry. I place her chin on my shoulder and rub her back.

"You have no idea how happy I am. I want to be yours forever, Luke. If I have to leave everything behind for you, I'm not even going to take a second look."

I lift her face from my shoulder and peer into her eyes. Tears gather at the corners of mine too. It's like hearing the bells of triumph ringing in my heart and feeling the clouds of joy underneath me. Words can't express how I feel and I can only show it by pressing my lips on Adeline's and kissing her until we both can't breathe.

When we break apart, my lips tingle with the warmth of her love and my body is wrapped in the embrace of our connection.

"So, you're coming with me?" I ask her.

"Of course."

I stand up and pull her to her feet. "Let's go. Right now.

We'll take the western route out of here and end up at the bus station."

We are almost to the door when Adeline pauses and asks, "What about Fena?"

"What about her?"

"We should tell her, right?"

"Tell me what?" Fena asks, standing in the doorway to the kitchen. She must have come in through the back door.

"We're leaving."

Fena frowns, spreads her hands and gives a silent "what?"

"Together," Adeline clarifies. She smiles at me, tangling her arm with mine.

Fena scoffs, probably not believing her ears. "Now? You're both leaving now?"

"Yes, Fena," I respond this time. "There's no point trying to build a future with Adeline in this chaos. I love her and I don't want to spend an uncertain life with her."

"But you can't just leave. There are wolves out now." Fena approaches us, the warning in her eyes raw. "They are going to find the two of you."

"We'll avoid them."

Fena takes a deep breath. "Honestly, I'm not trying to discourage you two. But we all know wolves are very active at night. The best cover is at day. By then, the enemy wolves would have gone to their pack. Don't risk this. You've got something special and a stupid mistake shouldn't ruin it."

I face Adeline to note what she thinks about that. The look in her eyes is enough to tell me she agrees with Fena. So do I.

"Okay, we'll spend the night. It'll give us a chance to rest."

Fena rolls her eyes. "Yeah, right. Rest." She walks to the couch and turns on the TV. "Sleep well," she says, putting way too much emphasis on the word "sleep."

Adeline and I grin at each other, slipping away to the

bedroom. Our future is hanging between us, sweet and beautiful, as we prepare for bed and climb in.

Adeline slips into my arms like it's natural. As if we've done it a hundred times before, and nestles into my chest. I stroke her arm gently, a peace I didn't know existed wrapping around my heart.

"We will have beautiful cubs," she says dreamily.

"Yeah," I chuckle, already imagining a little girl with dark hair and mischievous eyes. "I want three. You?"

Adeline chuckles. "Well, three isn't bad. I want a girl, though. I want to be able to name her Summer after my mom."

"Summer is a really beautiful name."

We don't speak for a while. It's still raining outside but the heavy pattering it had been making on the roof had now subsided. The smell of the rain floods the room, the tang of wet pine trees and cold night.

"Luke?" Adeline breaks the silence.

I drag my gaze from the door of the room, hating that I'm waiting for her brothers to break it down and steal her from me. Whenever something good is about to happen in my life, something else storms into it and ruins it. A few hours from now, I'll be on the road with Adeline, our past behind us, and I'm hoping, just hoping, that nothing will ruin the hours we have left.

Please let the curse that's hung over my life be broken.

I tighten the embrace and try to banish the thought out of my head. "Yes?"

"I want to hear about your family."

My gaze drops to her. But all I can see is her beautiful hair where it parts to frame her face. She trails her fingers on my chest, as if scribbling words on them.

"Really?" My voice is tainted with pain.

"Yes," she says, her voice hushed. "I want to hear how it happened."

The memory sneaks into my mind again. It's not something I want to welcome but for the sake of telling Adeline, I have to go over it. I shut my eyes and hear the fading drumbeats of my pack's festival, a celebration that had been taking place before the High Ridge wolves turned everything to an aching silence.

The smell of booze tingles my nostrils. It's not coming from the room but from that night, when I'd brought the beer to my nostrils and nodded to my mate that it was alcohol.

She didn't want to get drunk but her brothers kept passing off alcohol as nonalcoholic drinks to her because she couldn't smell. My mate had been born that way. She was the only wolf I knew who had no sense of smell.

"We were celebrating my brother's return," I explain to Adeline. "He left the pack for a while and came back. My dad saw the need to throw a party for him."

Adeline doesn't cut in. She listens with quiet attention, her steady heartbeat a soothing cadence against my body.

"That was when it happened. The High Ridge wolves came and crashed the party. They killed everyone, including my mate."

Adeline stiffens in my arms when she hears the word 'mate' and her heartbeat races, a little more than before. I stroke her hair and kiss her head.

"You had a mate?" she asks, trying to sound neutral even though her voice is strained.

"Yes."

Adeline raises her head to look at me. She studies me for a few seconds and then smiles. "You light up when you talk about her." The smile grows into a sad expression. Then she adds, "I'm sorry."

"I light up when I talk about you, too."

It's the truth. I'm not trying to make her feel less jealous or sorry for me. Jacqueline had made a comment about my face glowing whenever I talk about Adeline. She has this effect on me and has no idea how strong it is.

She puts her head back on my chest. "Tell me about your father. Did you love him?"

"I respected him. My father was this fearless wolf who didn't like people breaking his rules, not even his children. He was that strict. I'm not going to say my relationship with him was cordial but I feared him and he molded my brother and me into strong wolves."

"I don't know if my father still loves me." Adeline's voice quakes with ache. "He did, but he's different now. I was locked in a cellar for days and he didn't even..."

I stroke her arm again to console her. Her body trembles and her teardrops seep into my skin.

"It's okay. It'll soon be over. Where we're going, you won't even think about them."

Adeline moves away from me to rest on her elbow and peer into my eyes. "You promise?"

I put her hand on my chest and smile. "I promise."

I'm not going to break that promise, no matter what happens. Adeline has been through a lot and she doesn't deserve the memory of the past. I wish I had the power to steal all the ugliness that her family inflicted on her and only let her remember our moments together. It would be the greatest gift I would be giving her, I'm sure of it.

Adeline inches her face close to mine and kisses me on the lips. When she tries to pull away, I catch her mouth again, kissing her passionately. Our hot breaths mix, blending with pure love. Our souls connect, entangling in a sensational union.

Adeline is my joy and I don't need anything else. She's the healing I need, the thread closing up my torn heart.

It's ironic how we met because I wanted payback for what her family did to me but now, I'm willing to let everything go as long as I'll get to spend eternity with her.

When I stop kissing her, it's because my heart is overwhelmed with a single question.

"I want you," I murmur, breathless, exhilarated. "Will you be my mate? We'll get married tomorrow, along the way."

Without hesitation, Adeline nods, unable to control her tears. I kiss her again, moving my body close to hers and setting her back down on the bed.

Adeline spreads her legs to welcome me. I'm quickly lost in the warmth of her thighs, the freshness of her breath and the milkiness of her body. I ravage her mouth, covering her with my body, sliding the sweatshirt up her belly and slipping my fingers into her.

Adeline moans into my mouth as soon as my fingers part her pussy. She's already wet and the knowledge she's as turned on as I am is tinder to this explosive passion. I explore her deeper, tasting her constant moans. She shudders under me, heightens my pleasure.

I finger her gently, stroking her clit with my thumb. Adeline doesn't hide the impact it has on her. I stop kissing her to look at her reaction and see her eyes rolled back in her head. Her mouth is frozen on a gasp and the pleasure turns her neck rosy.

With my other hand, I put Adeline's hand over her head, clasping it while her other hand digs into my back. I fuck her with my fingers until she's writhing and whimpering, making me drunk with her scent and the way she gasps my name.

I grit my teeth. I want to be gentle. To pleasure her. To honor the commitment we've made to each other.

But then her hand wraps around my cock and tugs. "I need..." Addy moans, her eyelids at half-mast. "Make me yours, Luke."

My control snaps. "Mine," I growl as I flip her over, ramming myself back into her hot slickness with a resounding slap.

Addy arches her back and cries out, the sound building the inferno. I jerk her up so she's on her knees and she buries her face in the covers, her hands twisting in the material. I become blind with everything she incites. Passion. Fire. Possessiveness.

I drill and drive, losing all sense of anything but Adeline. My fingers dig into her hips with bruising intensity, but I can't stop myself. I want to brand her as completely as she has me.

Mine, my wolf roars.

A hurricane of pleasure wraps around my balls, my spine, turning my mind into a whirlpool of ecstasy.

"Luke, I'm going to—" Addy cries out as her orgasm rips through her. The walls of her pussy clamp around me, clenching and sucking.

Drawing me over the edge.

I chant her name as the climax shreds me. It tears through my groin, filling her hole with hot spend. I give her every drop, marking her as mine, lubricating our wild thrusts.

When the ripples finally release me, I fall to the side, bringing Addy with me. I'm breathing as if I just ran a marathon. My heart is a freight train in my chest.

Adeline chuckles and whispers, "That was great."

I pull her over and she cuddles me again. She's very warm now and I assume I feel the same way to her. Just thinking about what we did and how I'll do this with her forever brings a smile to my face.

"Where do you think we should go?" Adeline inquires.

"A city that's very far from here. We'll change our names, buy a house and start a family together."

"And you don't think they'll ever find us?"

"Adeline." I breathe deeply. "Stop thinking about them."

"It's just that I know my family. They'll search the ends of the world just to find me. I want to be with you, Luke, but we need to be smart about this. How do we cover our scents?"

"The perfume," I tell her. "We'll have to look for a seller, someone who is going to be selling it to us on a regular basis."

"Oh, that's a smart idea," Adeline comments.

I give her one last kiss and smile to myself again. I've got this worked out—I think.

"Luke?" Adeline speaks again. "Thanks for saving me."

I pull her in tighter. "No, you saved me."

CHAPTER 20
ADELINE

ena pounds on our door the next morning.

I stir in my sleep, awake enough to hear Luke leave the bed and open the door. The chirping of birds tells me it's already day.

"Fena, what's wrong?" Luke asks. His voice is faint, as though I'm still in a dream.

I'm too tired to even open my eyes. The warm bed under me is what I want to lay on forever—and Luke's chest. But he's no longer beside me. He's talking to Fena and her response forces my eyes open.

"They're still in the woods! You need to get out of here now!"

I sit up in bed, blinking rapidly to banish the sleep from my eyes. Fena looks alarmed, as though she saw something horrific outside. Luke looks back at me, his face squeezing into a worried expression.

"What are you talking about?"

Fena enters the room. She doesn't mind that I'm naked under the sheets and Luke is in his boxers. "Just get dressed!"

Luke grabs her arm before she can hurry out of the room and spins her around to look at him. "What's wrong?"

Fena glances in my direction before wriggling her arm from Luke's grip. "Her family. They're getting closer."

"Shit!" I cry, jumping out of bed. I grab Fena's sweatshirt and put it on. "They're following my scent, I'm sure of it."

"I don't think so. I masked your scent with the badger I killed last night. I think they know there's a pack in these woods. I'm not sure but I guess that's why they haven't gone back to their base."

I clutch Luke's hand. "We need to go."

Fena runs out of the room. I wait for Luke to get dressed and then we leave, just as Fena appears with a pair of trousers. She tosses it at me.

"Here. They should be your size. The badger's smell won't last long so you have to leave now."

"What about you?" I ask Fena. "What's going to happen to you?"

"You don't have to worry about me. Your scents will overpower mine. I'll fake a letter that says you should put the key under the mat when you leave and put it on my table. When they stumble on this cabin, they'll think I'm a kind human who took you in."

"Okay, we'll go now. Thanks, Fena." I hug the female wolf tightly. "You've been so kind to us."

I try to pull Luke out of the cabin but to my surprise, Luke doesn't move. I look at him and see he has his gaze on Fena. He's reluctant to leave.

"Fena, what's going to happen to the pack?"

"The pack? The Blood Borns?" Fena asks.

"Yes. If the High Ridge wolves know there's a pack here, they're going to attack you all. It's going to be a bloodbath."

"The Blood Born Pack should be the least of your worries,"

Fena says. "You need to get out of here before they get to the cabin. You know what Adeline's brothers will do to the two of you."

Luke turns his head and faces me. The look in his eyes provides the answer before I can even ask the question. He doesn't want to leave.

He's worried for the Blood Born pack.

"I'm sorry, Adeline, but I can't leave this pack to the High Ridge wolves. I can't watch innocent wolves die again." He kisses the back of my hand as he caresses my cheek with his knuckles. "You need to leave without me. I'll come and join you, I promise. We'll have that future but right now, I have to warn them that the High Ridge wolves are on their way."

I bite my lower lip and embrace him, much to his surprise. "I know. You've got a kind heart and that's why I love you so much. But I'm not going to leave here. I'm coming with you. We'll warn them together and then leave."

"But Adeline, this is a pack who wants your family dead. They're going to know you're not one of us," Luke says, his voice tense.

But I don't care. The most important thing is that we'll be warning a pack together. For years, I lived in the dark, oblivious of my family murdering entire packs and destroying people's lives.

But not this time. I'm not sitting back and letting them kill the Blood Born wolves. This is my choice and not even their probable hostility will dissuade me.

"We're doing this together, Luke, and you're not talking me out of it this time."

"Actually, Luke, maybe the Blood Born pack won't be a problem," Fena chips in.

"Why do you say so?" he asks, frowning.

"If Adeline warns them, then Arthur and the rest are going

to see her as a friend. They're going to appreciate the warning."

"Are you sure, Fena?" Luke shifts his weight, clearly uncomfortable with all of this. "I don't want anything to happen to Adeline."

Fena beams. "I'm sure. Now, hurry and leave this place. Go to Arthur and tell him the High Ridge wolves are coming."

Luke takes Fena's hand in his and squeezes it gently. "Thank you for everything."

"Go!" Fena slaps his arm, jolting him in the direction of the door.

However, before we walk out of the cabin, she says one last thing.

"Adeline?"

I wheel around. "Yes?"

"Your brother is a good guy." Her smile is sad. "If you ever get the chance, tell him he doesn't have to obey your family's rules. He's got a good heart and a chance to start afresh."

"So, are you going to tell me why Fena said that about my brother?"

The sun is out and so are we. I don't know how long we've been walking in the woods, crouching low to avoid chattering High Ridge wolves and dashing into opposite directions whenever we find one approaching us, but I know we've moving in circles and the Blood Born pack isn't anywhere in sight.

"Wait," Luke mutters, sinking behind a cluster of bushes as a wolf appears on a small bridge passing over a stream and sniffs the air.

I hide with him, watching the wolf come closer and closer. If the wolf doesn't see us, surely the pounding in my chest will alert him. Fear ripples through me as I recognize the wolf as

Kevin, one of Lawrence's friends. He's as crazy as my brother, but not in the Damian way. He'll be more than gleeful at the prospect of killing Luke, then promptly hurl me back to Lawrence.

A few seconds pass. It feels like an hour. Then Kevin turns around and goes back the way he came. It's only then that I let out the breath I've been holding.

"Let's go."

We walk out of the area. Luke stays ahead of me, his watchful gaze scanning the area and trying to pick out sounds of the enemy wolves. I can tell by the way his head slightly angles one way then the other as his nostrils flare every few seconds.

It's exhilarating watching his focused protection, more exciting that his hand never leaves mine as we travel through the woods. He'll keep me safe. Just like I will for him.

"So?" I break the silence.

"What?"

"The Fena and my brother thing."

"Oh, that." Luke doesn't look at me. "Do you want to hear that now?"

"Yes. It's rather strange that she thinks Jake's a good person. He is, but he's still my brother and he listens to Lawrence."

"She loved your brother," Luke confesses.

"Really? When did this happen?"

We continue walking while Luke tells me about Fena and Jake. I don't find it surprising that Jake was nice to a captive, or that Fena fell in love with him because of his kindness. Jake has always been a nicer brother. Back at the cellar, he was the one who stopped Lawrence and Damian.

"That's who he always talked about," I tell Luke, realization hitting me. "Jake talked about some girl the pack held captive and he never stopped. If you ask me, I'd guess Jake loved Fena."

Luke squeezes my hand but doesn't look back. "Maybe your brother has a heart after all."

A tent soon comes into view and in front of it is a buff wolf who has his claws stretched and milky eyes glaring our way.

"Hey, Jack," Luke calls out to the wolf before we get to him. "It's just me."

Jack's claws remain out and the scowl on his face fails to vanish at Luke's voice. "Who's with you?"

"She's a friend," Luke answers, carefully approaching Jack.

I follow him closely, clasping him hard. All my bravery is suddenly feeling naive and stupid. I'm the daughter of the High Ridge Alpha. They could try to kill me before we get a chance to explain why I'm here.

"She doesn't smell like us," Jack insists.

"Her name is Adeline and she isn't a threat. Please, Jack. I just want to talk to Arthur. I've got something very important he needs to know."

Jack regards us for a few seconds before withdrawing his claws and tilting his head in the direction of the tent. "You know how to get there, don't you?"

Luke nods. "Yes." He leads me towards the tent and turns to tell Jack something. "Be careful out here, Jack. The enemy wolves are closing in."

The milky-eyed wolf just grunts and says nothing. He doesn't seem to believe Luke —anyone should be scared at such news. Luke pulls me away. We find a narrow path behind the tent and follow it until Jack and the tent are out of sight.

"What's up with him? Those eyes?"

"He's blind, Addy, but he's the smartest wolf I've ever met. I just don't think he believes the High Ridge wolves will ever find the Blood Borns."

"And why is that?"

"They are under the protection of a High Wolf. I've never met him but the pack talks about how powerful he is."

I freeze in my tracks. "The High Wolf?"

Luke is astonished by my reaction. "Yes. Why? You know him?"

The memory of the night I overheard Lawrence telling his friend, Kevin, about a High Wolf and how he attacked my father slips through my mind. My brother never answered me when I asked who he was talking about, but hearing the name again has triggered my curiosity.

"My brother, Lawrence, talked about him some days after my mother's death. He said the High Wolf attacked my father and maybe my mother too."

Luke frowns. "What? That's impossible. Are you saying the High Wolf killed your mother?"

I shake my head. "I'm not sure, okay? Just a guess. But my family was rattled at that time and they kept talking about this High Wolf."

Luke rubs the back of my hand with his thumb as he faces me. This part of the woods is open and any wolf, whether Blood Born or High Ridge, can walk in on us.

"Adeline, ask any Blood Born wolf and they'll tell you the High Wolf is the best thing that happened to them. He's been hiding them in the woods for years and preparing them for battle against the High Ridge wolves. I don't think a wolf like that would kill your mother."

I take a deep breath. "Okay, maybe it's not him. I was just surprised to hear his name after such a long time."

Luke puts his hand around my shoulders and we begin to walk again. There's no point trying to doubt the saintliness of this High Wolf. After all, he's the head of this pack I'm about to warn, a pack that has become a family to Luke.

And Luke's family is mine, too.

CHAPTER 21
LUKE

The wolves of the Blood Born pack are sitting in a circle, listening to their leader, Arthur, talk to them when we arrive.

Arthur sees us first before the others. He breaks into a warm grin and ushers us to come forward as he says to his wolves, "Well, Luke is here, and I think with a friend."

I can almost note Adeline's hesitation to walk forward when I turn to look at her. Her eyes glimmer with fear and she grips my wrist a little roughly.

"It's okay." I pry her fingers just as they start to dig into my flesh. "They won't bite."

"Sorry," Adeline chuckles nervously.

Two wolves move aside so we can step into the circle. Arthur pulls me into a hug, kissing my forehead like I'm his child.

"Good to have you back, Luke."

It breaks my heart seeing him happy. For a moment, I don't want to wipe the excitement off his face, or his wolves' faces. They wear smiles, grins, and glints in their brightened eyes.

Arthur must have been telling them something exciting when we got here.

"I was just telling the pack about the High Wolf. He's on his way." Arthur's smile is the brightest I have ever seen.

And so are the High Ridge wolves.

"That's great, Arthur," I respond, hoping I don't sound somber.

Arthur glances at Adeline for the first time. Seems he was more thrilled to break the news to me than inquire who Adeline is. "Oh, hello," Arthur greets her. "Who's your friend, Luke?"

This is the moment that I've been waiting for but not in the way Arthur is waiting for the High Wolf's arrival. My heartbeat increases and I think about lying to them about Adeline. Will they welcome her with open hands?

"I'm Adeline," she replies before I can talk.

Arthur moves towards her. His nose flares once and I know he's already caught her scent. "You're not one of us. You're certainly not from here."

Adeline looks at me and I tell her with my eyes not to say a word. I've got this under control.

I lean in to whisper to the leader. "Can we talk somewhere else, Arthur?"

Arthur doesn't move an inch. The smile on his face slowly melts away. "Why? Whatever you have to say, say it in front of everyone. That's why we're a pack. We don't keep secrets."

I take a quick look at everyone. Some of the wolves are eager to hear what I have to say, their position leaning forward to hear me properly. Some of them don't wear an expression, their faces as bland as the atmosphere that has replaced the one of anticipation. But I know what's coming next when I tell them who Adeline is. The air is going to turn hostile and Adeline's life will be threatened.

So, I press her body closer to mine and answer, "She's a High Ridge wolf."

Instantly, every wolf in the pack jumps to their feet, claws shooting out in the blink of an eye. Growls rumble in their throats and their eyes gleam with raw malice. Even Arthur takes a step back, though his expression is more shock than anger.

"You brought the enemy into our pack?" he demands.

"Yes, but you need to hear what she has to say."

"Hear what she has to say?" A wolf bellows from the group. "She's one of them!"

"Yeah!" the others chorus, slashing their claws in the air and inching towards us.

I put a trembling Adeline behind me, turning in almost every direction that the wolves close in. They're not going to touch her, not on my watch. A growl starts inside me and my claws itch to shoot out.

"Listen to her, all of you!" I snarl at them. "Just listen!"

The wolves aren't listening. One of them charges towards us and as I flex my claws to attack him, but someone beats me to it. Arthur grabs the wolf by the neck and tosses him to the ground.

"Stay back, all of you! You only attack when I tell you to," the wolf barks at his people.

They withdraw to their former positions, but the intent to kill Adeline is still etched on their faces. I don't know if Adeline is weeping but her face is pressed to my back and something wet touches my skin.

Arthur looks at us, his dark eyes now fierce with rage. "Speak, woman! And God knows if you have nothing important for us, I'll order my wolves to tear you into shreds."

Adeline steps away from me. I still hold on to her and her glistening cheeks are a clear sign she's been crying.

"The High Ridge wolves are coming here," she answers, the

confidence returning to her voice. "They are going to attack the pack and I'm here to warn you all."

"T he High Ridge wolves?" Arthur asks, crossing his arms. It's hard not to note the sarcasm in his voice. "You mean, your family?"

"They are not family," Adeline quickly responds, wiping her cheek with the back of her hand. "A pack who slaughters other packs is not my family. Look, I know I was born as a High Ridge wolf but I'm not one of them. I'll never do what they do."

"This is a load of shit," Arthur snarls. "You're running out of time. My wolves are impatient."

"Arthur, let's kill her." Brena is the one speaking. Fena's friend has no idea what her friend did to save Adeline. "She'll serve as a warning to the High Ridge wolves."

"No!" I snap, stepping in front of Adeline to take over from where she stopped. "Adeline is telling the truth. She isn't like her family. I know her and I've seen her heart. It's true. The High Ridge Pack is closing in and she doesn't want any of you to get killed, that's why she's passing on this warning." I glare at every wolf, one by one. "Despite the risk it means for her."

Brena opens her mouth to talk again but Arthur quietens her with a raised finger.

"Really?" the leader says. A look of admiration now spreads across his face. "You trust her?"

"With my life," I reply.

Arthur nods, looking thoughtful. "Okay. You know what? Let's go into my tent. We have more to talk about."

The leader turns around and heads towards the region where the pack had pegged their tents. We follow, walking through the midst of snarling and enraged wolves. I catch the look in Brena's eyes and it's one that burns with raw anger.

Arthur's tent is the largest in the pack. It bears enough space for a sitting room, a kitchen and two bedrooms. He offers us seats—ladderback chairs made of polished wood. Adeline sits close to me and doesn't take her eyes off Arthur, not for a second.

I wouldn't either if I were in her shoes. The tent is a perfect spot to slaughter her, away from the gazes of other wolves and cubs. The Blood Born Pack was created for one thing—for every wounded wolf to become part of a bigger family, one filled with hope. Letting their younglings watch them as they kill the enemies isn't something Arthur wants.

"You're in love, aren't you?" Arthur says as he settles down in front of us.

Adeline and I exchange glances. I don't want to tell him the truth. Neither does she. But there's no hiding what he already knows.

"Yes," we say simultaneously

Arthur scoffs and shakes his head. "I never thought I would see this day again, one of my wolves falling for the enemy. I'm talking about Fena. She loved and, I think, still loves one of the High Ridge wolves."

Adeline and I exchange looks again. This time, I'm rather surprised Fena hasn't gotten over Jake. She spent time trying to convince me that my love for Adeline is my captivity. But deep down, she's still clinging to her love for Adeline's brother.

I level Arthur with a look. "If the High Wolf is coming, maybe he can decide." Surely he's a wolf of compassion. This pack wouldn't exist otherwise.

Arthur throws his head back to laugh. "So, you think you can talk to the High Wolf? Luke, that wolf is the most powerful one I've ever met. You can't just walk up to him and ask him to accept the enemy into our pack."

But I'm more determined than ever to prove to them that Adeline isn't like her family. "I don't care. Whatever it takes."

Just then, Jack runs into the tent, panting heavily like he just ran a million miles to get here. For a blind wolf, he does know how to barge into a room without ramming into something or someone.

"Arthur!" He says, almost breathless. "The High Wolf is here!"

Arthur springs to his feet. "Like right now?"

"Yes, but he's not yet in the camp. His first in command is here with the good news."

Arthur grabs Jack by the shoulders. "Did you see him? Do you know what he looks like?"

Jack looks confused. "No, I didn't."

It takes him a few seconds to realize he shouldn't have said that. The leader is so pumped with excitement that he isn't thinking straight.

"I have to go meet with him," Arthur says but before he can leave the tent, someone else enters.

It's the last person I'm expecting to see in a place like this. I shoot to my feet and from the corner of my eye, I see Adeline doing the same.

"Ryan?"

My next-door neighbor beams at me. His eyes are no longer creepy and there's an aura of confidence surrounding him.

"You're the High Wolf?" I blurt out.

"Oh, I wish. I'm just his right-hand man," Ryan answers. Then he sees Adeline. Mischief sparks in his eyes for a second before it vanishes. "She's here, I see."

A growl tangles in my throat. The realization of what Ryan is doesn't sit well with me. All this time, he'd been...

"You've been spying on me?" I ask, clenching my fist.

Ryan notes the action but it only brings an amused smile to his face. "Yes, I have. I was only doing the High Wolf's command."

"So, you two have met?" Arthur states the obvious. "Great! But Ryan, if I may ask, where is the High Wolf?"

"He's on his way but I came here to clear some things." Ryan's gaze settles on Adeline. "She can't be here when he arrives."

I scoff, holding Adeline by the hand. "Well, let's see you try to kick her out."

"Luke," Adeline murmurs to me. "I think I should go."

"No!" My tone is harsh and I really don't mean it but rage is surging through my body. "You're staying here and if anyone has a problem with it, they are the ones who should leave."

"You've always been stubborn!" Ryan grunts. "That's why the High Wolf asked me to watch you. You think before following orders and it's always been your downfall."

"The High Wolf asked you to watch me?" I laugh in mockery. "Now that's ridiculous! I don't even know who he is!"

"Oh, you know him alright!" Ryan slips his hands in his pockets. "He's always been there but your love for this woman has blinded you from seeing the truth."

"Watch your tone, Ryan," I growl. "The woman you're talking about is the person I want to spend the rest of my life with."

Ryan scoots closer to me and for a brief moment, I think he'll attack me. But his hands remain in his pockets. He stands in front of me, towering over me with his six-foot frame.

"She needs to leave," Ryan says firmly. "Her presence here is only going to make the High Wolf angry."

"She's staying."

Ryan cocks his head at Arthur. "And you're just going to

stand there and let him ruin the pack's meeting with the High Wolf?"

Arthur doesn't move an inch. He's clearly torn between listening to Ryan and letting Adeline stay, which is a worse choice because he risks being punished by this High Wolf.

Ryan looks at me again. "She isn't part of this pack."

I square my shoulders at him, not a trace of fear in me. "As long as Adeline is with me, she is part of this pack."

"No, she is not," a deep voice booms from the entrance of the tent.

A familiar voice.

I turn and the sight that greets me knocks the breath out of me. My knees buckle and my grip slides from Adeline's wrist. I stagger, lips quivering as I fight for words—any word!

Standing at the entrance of the tent in his black jacket and familiar creased pants is my father

My dead father.

Ready for the next installment in Black Diamond Alpha?
Check out ROGUE WOLF

ROGUE WOLF

I fell for a broken, wounded Alpha. One who sets my heart and body on fire.

And now I'm his captive.

After searching for most of his life, Luke's finally found where he belongs. Unfortunately, that pack will never accept me. To them, I'm a threat. One they're determined to crush.

We have the nights to lose ourselves to a love that changed everything. But by day, our enemy bloodlines define us.

I never wanted Luke to have to choose. Which means I might have to do it for him...

GRAB YOUR COPY HERE
https://mybook.to/RogueWolfTM

HAVE YOU READ THE FOREVER MATES PREQUEL?

As an exclusive for my subscribers,
you can download it for free!!

I've waited a long time for revenge. Worked toward this moment my whole life.

And it turns out Cassie is my ticket to justice. She's seen something she shouldn't have. And as a bounty hunter, I've been tasked with bringing her in.

Except everything I've worked for crumbles the moment I set eyes on her. One taste and everything is turned upside down. One night and my life is forever altered.

Turning Cassie over means she'll be killed. The need to protect what is mine clashes with the lifelong drive for justice. Can I have both?

Or will I have to choose?

CLICK HERE TO DOWNLOAD FOR FREE!

https://BookHip.com/PTNZMAL

ALSO BY TALA MOORE

SILVER MOON ALPHA

BLACK DIAMOND ALPHA

WILD HEART ALPHA

SHIFTER OBSESSION

FOREVER BOUND

APEX PACK

ABOUT TALA MOORE

Tala Moore loves all things paranormal and romance. Give her possessive alpha males, sassy heroines, and a love that refuses to be denied, and she's set for as long as she can disappear from the world (which is never as long as she'd like!).

Driven to create the same swoon-worthy experience for others, she pens the Forever Mates story world. Dive in and discover her penchant for unforgettable characters, steamy romance, and a HEA that will stay with you long after the story is finished.